FOREVER WITH A PRINCESS

HER ROYAL BODYGUARD
BOOK 3

MARGAUX FOX

UNTITLED

Her Royal Bodyguard Book 3

Forever with a Princess

1

Princess Alexandra checked her jacket pocket one last time, feeling the little box that nestled within. She ran her fingers over the hard edges and thought about what was in the box--and about what it meant. In the box were two very similar rings, a beautiful big sapphire that shone dark, glimmering blue, like the deepest ocean, with a diamond either side of it on a platinum band. There was also a more discrete ring, a platinum band with deep ocean sapphires alternating with diamonds. Both rings had been favorites of Alex's grandmother, who had adored sapphires. She had always said they were the most beautiful stone.

These particular sapphires were Kashmir

sapphires, known for their superior, fine, velvety cobalt-blue colour—unlike any other stone in existence. They were mined in the North Western Himalayas in 1884 and have become quite rare and valuable since then. Alex remembered being a child and marveling over the beautiful rings that her grandmother always wore on her wrinkled and arthritic fingers. She had always been fascinated by the stories behind them.

"There was an Indian maharaja who adored me, my darling. He used to say I was the most beautiful woman he had ever seen, that I was blue skies and sunshine with my blonde hair and blue eyes. It was 1947 when India became independent from the British royal family. I was twenty-one years old and traveling with your grandfather, whom I knew would be the next British king. The maharaja was so exotic, handsome, and always so charming. I fell in love with him straight away. But it was a fated love. It never could be. It took the form of friendship and he gave me jewelery often. Always Kashmir sapphires. He said they were the only thing in the world that were blue enough and beautiful enough to match my eyes."

The little Princess Alexandra would ask, "Are my eyes like Kashmir sapphires, Grandma?"

Her grandmother would always smile and say, "My darling, your eyes are just like my own. As blue as the most beautiful Kashmir sapphire in the world."

"But what happened to the maharaja?" Alex would ask.

"Oh, we had our own lives and our own worlds to return to, my darling. I knew I would one day become part of the British royal family. That was my destiny. His destiny was to marry an Indian girl of high standing. We remained friends over the years. Things were different in those days, my darling. So I just wear his rings, his sapphires, every day of my life. They are still with me now, and when I die, they will be yours. All my jewelry will be yours, but you will know that the sapphires are the special ones. The sapphires represent my real and true love. One day, Alexandra, I want you to wear them when you are in love. Not if and when you marry someone you are supposed to, but when you are really, truly in love and you feel it in every single part of you. You'll know—when it happens, you'll know. Your eyes will light up and shine like the Kashmir stones. I hope that in your lifetime there is a way to change what was, and that you will never have to marry out of duty. I hope that you get to marry out of love. I dream about what my life might have been like if I had married the maharaja. If such a thing had even been possible. I dream about the blending of our worlds and our cultures. Find your maharaja, my darling."

It was a story Alex's grandmother had told often, but only when she was alone with Alex. As though the young princess was the only one she really trusted, and perhaps she had been. Alex had always known that it wasn't a story to share.

The Kashmir sapphires, along with the rest of her grandmother's jewelry, had been locked away in keeping for Alex after her grandmother's death, and Alex was excited to have two of the rings in her pocket now.

Alex was in love now and her grandmother had been right—she did feel it in every part of her being. In the same way that her grandmother had fallen for someone whom she wasn't supposed to, Alex had too. But, so many years later, Alex was finding a way to make it work.

Alex took a deep breath as she settled in to the back of the Range Rover, on her way to the hospital to bring Erin home.

Alex would marry a woman, this incredible

woman who made her smile every day. This incredible woman who had saved her life.

Alex was strong. She would and could change things for the future. She would be a role model for so many young people who questioned their sexuality. She would have the first same-sex royal wedding. Alex owed it to her grandmother and she owed it to all the people who were hiding their true selves. She owed it to herself.

Alex turned to Sergeant Joanne Davis, her bodyguard, "Please wait outside."

"Hey," she said almost shyly as she walked into Erin's hospital room, seeing that Erin was fully dressed and lounging on the hospital bed. It was the first time Alex had seen her in her own clothes since she had been rushed into the hospital weeks earlier.

Erin smiled widely at her and Alex felt shivers run through her body. She was still so affected when Erin smiled at her like that. Alex had never had that feeling before—of someone being so happy to see her.

Alex still hadn't forgotten the panic she had

felt throughout that day, fearing that Erin would die. Alex had been so scared, thinking that her life had been too good to be true and that was why the most important thing to her would be taken away. She still didn't know how she would have coped if she had lost Erin.

But she hadn't and that is what mattered. Erin was fine. She was recovering well. She was coming out of the hospital. She would be absolutely fine.

Erin stood up and embraced her, and Alex melted into her arms. Erin felt thinner and Alex made a mental note to feed her up when they got home. She couldn't wait to get her home.

But first, she had something important to do.

"Um..." she mumbled, breaking Erin's embrace. Alex was usually so eloquent and gifted with all the words, but suddenly, and in the most important moment in her life, her words deserted her.

Alex was wearing a dark red dress that came to just above the knee, so she took a moment to hitch it up a little and then knelt on one knee, fumbling for the tiny box in her pocket, which she pulled out and opened.

She was still surprised by the brilliance of the stones, even under the stark, flourescent lights of the hospital room. The Kashmir sapphires shone and the diamonds sparkled next to them.

"So, I wanted to do this properly. But for someone who is very used to speaking publicly and addressing the whole world, I'm not doing a great job here, during the biggest moment of my life."

Alex took a deep breath and looked up at Erin, who smiled back with tears in her eyes.

"You have come in to my life and changed everything. I never thought in a million years that I would have the bravery to come out and live authentically, but you have made that possible for me. You have given me the belief in myself that I needed. You are the strongest, most noble, most incredible person I have ever met. You have saved my life in every way that a person can be saved. I know I am asking for a lot. I know being with me has not been easy and will never be. I know I am asking you for huge sacrifices by asking you to become part of the royal family. But I want you by my side for the rest of forever. I want you with me as I become queen. Sergeant Erin Kennedy, will you do me the immense honor of becoming my wife?"

Erin smiled and pulled Alex up in her arms,

kissing her deeply. Alex felt the world stop as Erin's kiss ran through her whole body. Erin's strong arms protected her. She urged Alex to sit down on the edge of the hospital bed, and then took the ring box and placed it next to her. She took Alex's hands in her own and looked into Alex's eyes.

"Absolutely yes. I'm with you. Right with you. Forever. Through it all. You are already my queen." Erin smiled at her. "Right. These rings look a bit more royal than the last one you gave me."

She took the ring with the smaller band and the bigger sapphire and raised it to Alex's left hand. It slid easily onto Alex's finger—she had had the band made smaller to fit her.

Alex looked at it happily, as though the moment were magical. She took the other ring from the box and slid it onto Erin's hand. She had resized the band to make it a bit bigger, although she'd had to guess about the size that would fit Erin. Alex breathed a sigh of relief as it fitted perfectly.

"God, Lex, this ring is stunning. It is so right. So me. It was your grandmother's?"

"Yes." Alex smiled. "It was. Both rings were. She said that sapphires represent true love, and I was supposed to wear them when I felt truly in love."

Erin's eyes were watching the ring as the stones glowed in the light. "These sapphires, they match your eyes."

"So you can always think of me when you look at them." Alex felt warm inside.

Erin laughed and pushed her back on the bed, kissing her. "I fucking love you, future Mrs. Kennedy."

"I fucking love you too," Alex laughed. Future Mrs. Kennedy sounded perfect.

They chose to exit the hospital via the main entrance and the press had been invited. Alicia had popped in to quickly fix Erin's hair and makeup. Erin had on a crisp, button-down shirt in dark blue, which set off the deep red of Alex's dress.

They held hands as they walked out of the hospital smiling. The security team had cleared a channel for them. Cameras snapped madly.

"Alexandra!"

"Erin!"

"Princess!"

The press called loudly to them and they posed for photos before Alex began to speak.

"I would like to make a short statement." As always happened when Princess Alexandra began to speak, everyone fell silent.

"Sergeant Erin Kennedy saved my life. Both in taking a bullet that was meant for me and in giving me the space to come out and be authentically myself. I will forever be in her debt. She is the strongest, most genuine and most caring partner I could ever wish for. In almost losing Erin, I realised for sure how much she meant to me. That day, when Erin got shot, is a day that will haunt me forever. I am eternally grateful to my security team for taking down the threat and the person responsible. I am eternally grateful to the hardworking staff of this hospital for saving Erin's life. I would also like to take this opportunity to announce my engagement to Erin. Our relationship has been a first for the royal family and our wedding will be, too. Things are changing for the better in our country and I am honored to be a part of it."

Alex followed her announcement with her best photo smile and Erin put her arms around the princess from behind. She felt the familiar rush through her body and took Erin's left hand and her own left hand and positioned them over her collarbone, so the photographers could get pictures of their rings.

Alex smiled to herself, looking down at her own neatly manicured, delicate fingers next to Erin's strong fingers and natural short nails. Erin's touch burned through her, and she wanted Erin to take her there and then. *Stop it Alex, for god's sake*, she mentally scolded herself.

The questions from the journalists began.

"Ma'am, huge congratulations. Can you tell us about the rings?"

"The stones are Kashmir sapphires, given to my grandmother by the Maharaja of India in 1947."

"Sergeant Kennedy, how are you feeling?" Erin's arms tightened around Alex, and Alex felt the strength in her that she so adored.

"I'm feeling elated, thank you. I feel like the luckiest woman in the world to get to marry Princess Alexandra. The princess is what this country, and indeed the world, needs. She is everything that is good in the world and I am eternally grateful to have the opportunity to love her. And, if you meant physically, I am doing well. I am very grateful to the hospital staff who have worked on me. I am recovering well and there will be no lasting damage. Might just need Alexandra to run around after me for a few weeks."

Everyone laughed.

"Ma'am, Your Highness, what are your wedding plans? Will the Church be on board with a same-sex wedding?"

"Our wedding plans are still in their early stages. When we have more definite plans, I will release details. Thank you very much."

Alex wrapped up the questioning, ignoring further pleas of questions, and plastered her best smile back on, taking Erin's hand and leading her to the Range Rover.

Quickly they were inside and driving away, and the noise from the press and the flashes from the cameras were over.

"God," Erin tipped her head back and closed her eyes for a second. "I will never get used to that. I don't know how you do it. You are so good at knowing what to say and knowing how to make them stop."

Alex put her hand on Erin's thigh. "You sounded like a media pro yourself there. All your training with the palace PR team is definitely paying off."

Erin laughed. "Getting there. Hopefully. They put some real effort into training me before they let me loose in public."

"I think that was wise. Can't be too careful. God knows what you would have said otherwise!"

"Yeah, something like, 'Oh I feel so lucky! I get to do hot and dirty things with the precious and pure Princess A.'"

"Oh my god, you are *unbelievable*!" Alex reached across and punched her arm.

"Careful, careful. I got shot, remember? Saving your life! I'm a hero!"

"Never going to let that one go are you, Kennedy?"

"Never, Future Mrs. Kennedy!"

Alex looked across at Erin's green eyes, which were glittering darkly. It had been lonely sleeping alone, while Erin had been in the hospital. She couldn't wait to have Erin home.

2

Erin awoke the next morning to the sunlight filling their bedroom. Alex must have been up early and opened the curtains.

She felt disorientated just for a second, but it felt so good to be home in her own bed and no longer in the hospital. It still felt crazy that this huge, luxurious bedroom was hers. God, she had missed it during the weeks she had been trapped in the hospital room. Erin threw the covers off and stretched out, languorously luxuriating in the feeling of the sunlight on her skin. Her body felt slightly different and she wondered if that was a post-surgery thing. She'd been left with a scar on the back of her ribcage. It wasn't massive, but the skin around it felt tight.

Erin was very aware of it. She also knew that there were scars inside that were still healing, and she wondered if that was what felt so different. Erin moved her hand to the site of the wound and ran her thumb over the raised skin. It ached a bit, the area where the bullet had entered. The surgeons had had to cut through the muscles between her ribs to gain entry, so they could repair the damage done by the bullet. Erin had broken her ribs once, years ago, falling off a horse . The pain and aching reminded her of that time.

It had been intensely painful during the first week in the hospital. Any movement had hurt. Talking hurt only a little. Laughing hurt a lot. But since then, things had begun to gradually improve. Erin was young, fit, and healthy. There was no reason she shouldn't heal quickly and be back riding soon.

She looked at the fourth finger of her left hand, where the sapphire and diamond band sat. Marriage wasn't something she had ever seriously contemplated before. But suddenly here she was, engaged to the future queen, and serious contemplation was definitely necessary. This was a huge, massive life choice. The potential options for her future with the princess had been discussed in meetings with the king and his royal advisors. Erin had known that a hypothetical engagement had been discussed, but she hadn't expected that moment with Alex and the Haribo gummy. She had seen the fear and the love melding in Alex's eyes—fear that she had almost lost Erin and love because she hadn't. And because she did love Erin. Absolutely and entirely, as Erin did her. Erin had never been in a relationship where it felt like this. Sure, she had been in love before; she had had girlfriends before; but this intensity was different. It was like next-level love. She needed Alex like she needed oxygen. Alex was right, in that everything became complicated just by being with her. And it was—hugely complex. But underneath everything else, they were just two women who loved each other. Erin figured that as long as they had that, everything else would be okay.

She could hear the birds outside and wondered where Alex was.

Erin had missed her so much while she had been in the hospital. Alex hadn't left her side during the first forty-eight hours. Instead, she had slept in the chair next to Erin's hospital bed. As soon as Erin felt well enough to tell Alex to go home and sleep, she had said just that. And after an argument where Alex had pouted and had asserted that princesses always get their own way, she had finally conceded and had gone home to sleep.

The power dynamics were still shifting. Erin was adjusting from working *for* the princess to being *with* the princess. Alex was accustomed to telling people what to do and to getting her own way. Nobody ever challenged her. She was hugely powerful.

While Erin never wanted to be in a relationship where she was controlling in any way, a part of her really got off by challenging Alex and seeing Alex do as Erin chose.

Erin was gradually getting more confident about airing her views and opinions when she disagreed with Alex. While they were often initially met with Alex's pout, Erin was finding that her ideas were also met with a curiousity in Alex's blue eyes. She would watch as Alex assessed what she had said. Contemplated her words, and then opened her sharp mind to Erin's opinion.

Alex, Alex, Alex—I'm obsessed with her.

Erin thought about those blue eyes and imagined

them here with her, looking at her obediently, doing whatever Erin wanted her to do. Erin found her right hand making its way slowly down her naked body, running over her abdominal muscles, finding her hipbone, tracing down over her groin, reaching the wetness between her legs. She closed her eyes and bathed in the sunshine, letting her fingers trail lazily between her slick folds. Teasing herself with her fingers. Running them lightly around her clit.

"Hey you, starting without me?"

Erin's eyes flashed open and she suddenly saw Alex in front of her. She smiled. "Where did you come from? You must have snuck in quietly!"

"I was just out with Audrey. I thought I would let you sleep in. Had I known what you were really up to, I might have stayed."

Alex was wearing a light, pale-pink sundress that was very "Home Alex," as opposed to "Public Alex." It was loose on her and Erin could see her nipples rising prominently under the fabric, and knew she wasn't wearing a bra.

"So, Sergeant Kennedy, what were you thinking about, lying here touching yourself?"

"I was just thinking about how hot it is when beautiful princesses do exactly as I tell them to."

"Had a lot of princesses, have you?" Alex's eyes glittered as she teased Erin.

"Oh, wouldn't you like to know?"

"What would you like your princess to do for you today?"

Erin sat up and made her way over to sit at the edge of the bed. She worried momentarily about the postsurgical pain she was still feeling in her ribs, but she adjusted her position so it didn't hurt. "I would like my princess to take her dress off and kneel between my legs, for a start."

Alex obediently began to pull the dress up over her head. As Erin suspected, she wasn't wearing underwear—as she often didn't when they were at home. It drove Erin absolutely crazy knowing that Alex was nude under her dress.

Erin's eyes watched the lines of Alex's lovely body lit up in the morning sunlight. Alex's narrow ribcage and the bit of her stomach that dipped in just below it. Alex's thick, blonde pubic hair that looked like strands of pure gold in the light. Alex's breasts that always looked surprisingly round against her petite body. Erin thought Alex looked like a dancer because her body moved with an innate grace. Alex dropped to her hands and knees and crawled across the floor, arriving on her knees —between Erin's legs.

Watching her on all fours, crawling, with her breasts swaying slightly, Erin couldn't take her eyes off her. Alex rocked back on her knees and looked obediently up, from between Erin's legs.

"What would you like me to do now?" she asked, her voice dripping with sweetness.

God, she is too good at this.

Erin moved her right hand to Alex's exquisite ashy blonde hair that was loose about her shoulders and wove her fingers into it, tangling it into her fist.

"Make me come using your mouth and fingers." Her eyes met Alex's and her hand pulled Alex's head in towards her. She didn't take her eyes off Alex's face as her eyes closed and her mouth opened for Erin's clit. Her lips closed around Erin's clit and she sucked gently, and Erin felt her clit swelling into the heat of Alex's mouth. She thought she might come right there and then, purely at the attention of Alex's mouth and the sight of Alex between her legs, but she held her orgasm at bay and relaxed into Alex's mouth, while her hand still held a handful of Alex's hair.

Erin's passion for Alex made her want to grab

tightly and grind into Alex's mouth, and orgasm within seconds. But she didn't. Erin had patience and she wanted to wait. She knew it would be better if she waited.

She watched as Alex relaxed into her task, her tongue moving in long strokes, then short swirls, then her lips enveloping part of Erin. She alternated between sucking gently and sucking harder and more intently. Alex's eyes were closed and she was lost between Erin's legs, purely there for Erin's pleasure. However, it also looked like Alex's own pleasure came from giving orally to Erin.

Erin felt Alex's right hand suddenly, pushing at her wetness, teasing and playing.

Oh, fuck.

She felt Alex's fingers push deep inside her and curl round straight to her G spot and she knew it was all over. Erin's head tipped back and she tightened her grip in Alex's hair. She called out loudly as her orgasm rushed through her. She felt it ripple from the white hot centre between her legs —right through every single inch of her body. Erin felt her body relax and let go of the tension it had been holding, and she let go of her grip on Alex's hair. She finally opened her eyes and saw Alex smiling at her.

"That was fucking incredible."

Alex held Erin's gaze, taking the fingers of her right hand and putting them in her mouth. Slowly sucking and licking every last trace of Erin's orgasm from them.

"You filthy bitch," Erin murmured, not looking away for a second.

"We both know you wouldn't have it any other way." Alex's steely blue eyes burned into Erin's as she sucked her fingers one last time then removed them from her mouth, looking satisfied.

Erin had thought she had had good sex before, but with Alex it was always more. Their connection was so intense and raw that she knew nothing else would compare.

She felt a rush of something so primal that she knew she needed to fuck Alex immediately. She moved quickly to stand up and move behind Alex, pulling her up and throwing her upper body roughly forward over the bed.

Alex's ass was round and bent over in front of her. Erin moved each of her legs so that they were parted wider.

"Take your weight on your feet and keep your face to the bed. I want your beautiful ass in the air for me."

Alex looked incredible as the sunlight hit her ass and her icy blonde hair splayed over the bed. She was a million miles away from the princess she had to be each day.

Erin ran her hands over Alex's sides where the lines of her body dipped in before splaying out roundly. Erin's hands ran over the pale globes of Alex's ass and Alex's body shivered with desire in front of her.

Erin's hands ran down the outsides of her thighs and her finely muscled calves and then they ran back up the inside. Goosebumps spread right across Alex's thighs as Erin's hands trailed up the inside of them.

Erin's right hand reached the wetness that was beginning to trickle down Alex's inner thigh.

"Mmmm, pretty turned on here, aren't we, Princess?"

She smeared her finger through the juice and then put it to Alex's lips, and Alex began to suckle on Erin's finger, tasting her own desire. Erin felt Alex's want and need, from her mouth on Erin's finger and how she sucked it.

She took her hand back to pull aside the cheek of Alex's ass with her left hand and trail the fingers of her right hand down slowly over the rim of Alex's asshole, and the folds of her wetness.

Alex moaned helplessly in front of her, completely on display. Completely turned on by being displayed.

Her body felt electrically responsive to Erin's fingers. Just a touch on Alex's clit and Erin could feel Alex's body answering her.

Erin ran her fingers up and down a teasingly few times, knowing that she really didn't have the patience to make Alex wait. She had missed Alex while she had been in the hospital. She thought perhaps they had kept her there too long—longer than if she had been a normal person who had been shot. Extra precautions must be taken when you are the princess's girlfriend.

As a result, Erin felt like their bodies needed to reconnect sexually. The drive between them had always been so passionate and strong, which meant that a couple of weeks without that kind of touch had been too long for both of them.

Erin's ribs were beginning to ache. Perhaps she had overdone things too soon after surgery. However, she was way too lost in the sex to stop and feel any pain.

She plunged her fingers into Alex, curling them downward and finding Alex's G-spot with her fingertips. She padded against it, pressed against it, and began to fuck Alex with her fingers. Alex's body leapt at the penetration and pushed back at her, wanting more. She groaned loudly as Erin added a third finger and Erin felt hot liquid gush out, running down Alex's inner thighs in appreciation.

There was always something so satisfying about fucking Alex like this. Alex craved rough penetration and Erin was more than happy to give it. Alex's body had early on in their sex life begun to squirt for Erin's fingers. It was a level of release that Alex would beg her for.

Watching her like this, coming undone and gushing repeatedly for Erin's fingers, was a pleasure she never ever tired of.

Her thumb moved to Alex's clit and as her fingers moved in and out, fucking her, her thumb slid firmly back up and down over her clit. Erin held her hip tightly with her left hand.

Erin felt Alex tightening around her fingers and she screamed as she came hard in a pool of wetness. Erin felt Alex's body pulsing on her fingers as her orgasm rode through her. Alex's legs collapsed under her and she fell forward onto to the bed.

Erin looked at her for a second, Alex's body quivering post-orgasm as she lay there in front of her.

Erin got on the bed, taking care not to hurt her own ribs or Alex, and lay quietly on top of her, her own breasts squashed against Alex's back. She was so much bigger than Alex that she covered her completely. She put her hands on top of Alex's and wove her fingers in with Alex's.

She kissed Alex's hair, her neck, and the side of her face. She moved her lips to Alex's ear.

"You are the most beautiful woman I have ever seen," she whispered.

Erin felt a shiver run through Alex's body beneath her as she tenderly kissed Alex's ear.

"I love you."

3

Alex made her way to a meeting with her father. There was a lot to discuss.

"Alexandra, lovely to see you. You look radiant today."

"Thank you, Father." Alex sat down across the desk from him. He was alone today, without his right-hand man. *He looks older, perhaps,* Alex thought, as she pondered him. His face looked weathered and his eyes, the same blue as her own, looked tired.

"I know we haven't had a chance to discuss what happened yet, so I thought today could be the day. First, I am relieved that Sergeant Kennedy is recovering well. What she did on that day for you—and indeed, what she did for the monarchy

—constitutes an outstanding act of bravery, heroism and courage in extreme danger. I would like to award her the George Cross to recognise her gallantry, and in due course I will have a ceremony arranged to award it to her. She has saved the life of a future monarch while risking her own, which is the most noble act a civilian can perform. Her devotion to the monarchy, and to you, is second to none. You have chosen your partner most wisely, Alexandra."

"Thank you, Father. I'm sure Erin will be overwhelmed and most grateful to receive such a high honor."

"Concerning what happened and the threats upon your life, Rob has assured me that the members of that particular extremist group have been jailed. They will no longer be an issue. Obviously, the press has been given a version of events, which makes it look like these were the actions of a lone, right-wing extremist, targeting you for homophobic reasons. We still have our suspicions about my brother Arthur's involvement, but we need to keep that well away from the media."

"They can't find anything linking the shooter to him?" Alex asked.

"No. Unfortunately, we have no evidence. So at this point, we really don't know."

"What do you think, Father?"

"Do I think my own brother conspired to have my daughter murdered? What a question I have to ask myself. I wish I could say he would never do that, but I don't trust him at all. My thought is that he is involved on some level. To what extent, I don't know. I don't think he would ever get his own hands dirty, but would he conspire to murder you? God, I sincerely hope not. If they had succeeded in killing you, would they have come after me next? That's entirely possible."

"Ah, Alexandra, as you well know, being the monarch or next monarch comes with huge responsibility, an incomparable level of duty, and at times, great risk. You faced risk during the last few months, and you faced it bravely and head on. Your bravery in continuing to appear in public and continuing to push your LGBTQ youth charity did not go unnoticed. Your popularity with the people has gone through the roof. The children in the schools you have visited love you. The people love you, and they also love Sergeant Kennedy—all the more so for her act of heroism. You two are the golden couple of the moment. You have the nation behind you. As you know, I was entirely behind your proposal announcement and would like us to look forward to your wedding. A royal wedding for the golden couple is exactly what this nation needs right now."

Alex nodded. "Yes. I think this is our moment."

"So, if you are in agreement, I think we move relatively quickly to put things in place for the royal wedding. I must tell you, Alexandra, your mother isn't happy about it. She will go along with it and attend—she has no choice—but like before, she may be your biggest challenge." Alex looked straight ahead, stoically. Her relationship with her mother had always been bad, even before she came out. Nothing Alex did would ever please her mother and she knew that. It didn't make it easy to accept, but Alex knew she could never win her mother's approval.

"The other problem we have is the Church. I want you to have a think, Alexandra, about what you want to do about the Church. As the monarch, I am Head of the Church. When I die, that title will pass to you along with the crown—unless, of course, we put changes in place to separate the monarchy from the Church. I know you will do your duty to the Crown, but I wanted to offer you an option. The current advice is that it may be time for the monarchy to split from the Church, particularly in the event that the next monarch will be part of a same-sex marriage. I know that the royal wedding is usually held in a cathedral, and is a religious affair. Now, I have had to do some thinking about this one. We could push for that. We could push for a same-sex religious ceremony. However, I'm not sure it is what you want--and it almost certainly isn't what the Church wants. What I am telling you is that there may be another option."

"Have a think about it, Alexandra," her father continued. "I believe you will bring changes to the Crown and I believe you are absolutely the right person for the job. I'm perhaps old-fashioned in my own views, but our world is changing and I am not naïve about that. The only way for the monarchy to survive will be to move with the times, and my advisors and I are of the same opinion that you are a gift to the Crown. You are what the people want. You have an almost universal appeal, and I have to admit that I have been surprised by the popularity of Sergeant Kennedy—a commoner—as your partner. They love that she isn't from noble bloodlines, and surprisingly, there seems to be a really positive response to the fact that she is also a woman."

"Yes, I thought so too." Alex nodded. "I spent so many years thinking that I could never come out because I feared the public's response. Yet, aside from my mother and extremists who are trying to kill me, it has been overwhelmingly positive."

"I'm happy for you, Alexandra. You deserve a happy life and a partner you love. I am glad that the world has changed enough to allow you that. There will be difficulties, of course. I don't doubt that in some countries you visit, you will need to be ready to encounter hatred because of your sexuality. We will need to be a lot more cautious and think carefully about how best to manage those visits before you head out."

He pulled open the drawer of his desk and produced a whiskey bottle and two crystal glasses. He started pouring.

"Have a drink with me, Alexandra."

Alex had always hated whiskey, although the smell of it reminded her of her father. She remembered the smell on his breath when she was a child. Alex smiled and nodded.

"Cheers!" he said, raising one glass and pushing the other across the desk toward her.

Alex picked it up, then raised it to clink in the air with her father's glass. "Cheers!" she said, and they both took gulps of the amber liquid. Her face screwed up as she felt the heat of the whiskey burn down her throat.

"To the future of the Crown," he said, taking another big gulp. Alex sipped this time, much more cautiously.

"Also, Alexandra, I am not getting any younger. I want to give you a full-time advisor of your own to begin to prepare you for the Crown. I know we have spoken about this before and you had said you wanted a woman. I have had someone I think will be suitable and she has been specially chosen. I want you to meet with her. If you think she would be a good match, then she will begin to work with me—shadowing my activities in preparation for when you take over."

Alex was surprised for a second, but didn't let it show on her face. Her father wasn't that old. She hadn't expected to take over any time soon.

"Of course, Father. Have a meeting arranged for me."

He nodded and refilled his whiskey.

Was it strange that he was openly drinking in the middle of the day?

A week later, Alex was in the lounge while Erin was out at the stables, spending some time with Shimmer and Vic. She was desperate to ride again, but despite her best efforts to pretend that she was fine, both Alex and Vic could tell that Erin was still struggling with pain from the surgery. Her body was still healing. It would take time until she could ride again.

For now, Vic was riding Shimmer and Erin was relegated to watching. Alex knew how frustrated Erin was, but neither Alex nor Vic would let her ride until they thought she was sufficiently recovered—enough so that she wouldn't do herself any further harm.

Jess bustled into the lounge, her little legs moving as fast as usual, and her white, button-down shirt straining around her large breasts.

"Morning, Ma'am," Jess smiled and spoke quickly, all at once. "I have your mail here. You have a meeting with Julia Wilding, organised by your father's office, at 11am. Where would you like to take the meeting? I could have an early, light lunch prepared for you on the terrace. The weather is lovely today!"

"Thank you, Jess, that would be lovely. I will receive Julia on the terrace."

"Of course, Ma'am." Jess dropped the mail on the table, next to Alex's coffee, and practically dashed out of the room. Alex wondered how someone could be as busy as Jess always was. Jess made sure everything ran smoothly for the princess at all times, but it intrigued Alex that Jess herself always operated at one hundred miles an hour.

Alex picked up the mail. As usual, there were three piles, because Jess sorted mail into *important*, *things you might enjoy reading*, and *things you might not want to read*. Jess read through all the fan mail herself, to categorize it, although Alex had asked to have access to all the mail, rather than not. It was impossible to be as famous and publicly "out" as Alex was, and not to receive hate mail. Sometimes she read bits of it. Often, she took it straight to the hearth without reading it and burned it in the fireplace. There was something therapeutic, purely in the act itself.

Your words cannot hurt me.

The positive fan mail, Alex always made an effort to read. Then she either replied herself, or had Jess reply on her behalf. There had been a lot from children or parents since she had started Rainbows. They praised Alex's bravery in coming out, as well as the work she was doing around LGBTQ visibility, education, and representation. They begged Alex to visit their school, or sometimes even their towns or houses!

There were heartwarming letters, saying that Alex had given them the courage to live authentically, or that Alex had helped them realize that they weren't alone—which had saved their lives. Those letters were Alex's favorites. She always read them in their entirety and tried to reply herself if she could.

Often, she would sit with Jess and work through a load of responses. Alex would dictate what she wanted to say while Jess would type busily. Later, Jess would bring the printed letters for Alex to sign before she mailed them.

It was times like this when Alex loved her position. Being able to do good and to change people's lives for the better was a great use of her power. Alex could get entirely on board with this mission.

She only had a half-hour this morning before she was due to meet Julia Wilding, her potential Royal Advisor, so Alex took the pile of hate mail straight to the hearth, struck a match, and burned it. She enjoyed the sweet, yet bitter, smell of the smoke. The letters burned and Alex smiled.

You will not hurt me.

She flicked through the good fan mail and decided that she didn't have time to go through it properly that morning. She would schedule time to go through it with Jess later.

She picked up the pile labeled important. Today there was only one envelope in it. This mail Jess didn't go through. The envelope was still sealed with a wax-stamped crest in red. Wax sealing was something that had been done since the 16th century and some nobles still favoured the ancient art of hand-writing letters with fountain pens and sealing envelopes with wax. The handwriting on the front was elaborate and all big loops in expensive looking ink on expensive looking paper.

Princess Alexandra
Private and Confidential
From Lady Annabelle Delacourt.

Alex had recognised the handwriting, but when she read Annabelle's name, she jolted. What on earth would Annabelle be writing to her for? She hadn't seen Annabelle since that party where things had gotten awkward and Alex had felt herself panicking and falling apart. She felt so much more together now. She knew that her meltdown in front of Annabelle had been caused by her stress following the threats against her life. But Alex felt so much stronger now, in every way. She ripped open the envelope, lifted out the heavy paper with the beautiful handwriting, and began to read.

My Dearest Alexandra,

I don't know how to adequately put in to words how sorry I am for everything, but I am going to try.

Firstly, I apologise profusely for my behaviour towards you at the party at the Duke of Rangeaux's. I had been having some difficulties in my marriage and I had had too much to drink. My behaviour towards you was completely out of order. I am so very sorry if I put you in a difficult position.

I also want to apologise for what happened between us years ago. Well, not for what happened—not for a second do I regret being with you—but I want to apologise for the way I left you.

I was so conditioned to heterosexuality. I was so

absolutely conditioned to look for a suitable (very wealthy and titled) husband.

I honestly wish that I had been braver and able to act on what was real. Because what happened between us was absolutely real. I know you used to tell me you loved me and I never said it back. Well, I just want you to know that I loved you too, Alexandra. Absolutely and in every way.

I married Rupert for who he was and the type of lifestyle he could give me. I realise now how pathetic that sounds, but it is what so many women have done over the years and still do. I never loved him. I never wanted him. But I built a life with him, and here I am years later.

I do not regret our children for a second, but it has become entirely clear to me that our marriage is empty and dead. (And perhaps always has been). I do not want to live that life anymore.

Rupert is seeing someone else. Some hot young thing whose body hasn't been marred by three pregnancies. It feels on some level like the most predictable thing in the world. This is what happens with wealthy and entitled men, right?

They start fucking the nearest hot young thing. Their wives know about it, but they stay, regardless.

They don't want to give up their status and their lifestyle, right?

Well, not this time. We have agreed to divorce amicably and create two stable homes for the children, of whom we will share custody.

I'm telling you this with no expectation, Alexandra. I entirely respect your engagement to Sergeant Kennedy and I just wanted to tell you congratulations, and that I wish you both nothing but the best.

What I would like is to make amends and to rebuild our friendship.

For so many years, our friendship has been damaged by my actions all those years ago. But, we had such a good friendship. I would love to bring that back, and to be there for you to help you prepare for your wedding.

I wanted to tell you that honestly, the way you have chosen to live your life and to come out publicly has inspired me. It is probably what made me brave enough to leave Rupert.

There is no pleasure in a loveless marriage.

Alexandra, it would mean the world to me if you would agree to meet me and reconsider our friendship. I would also like to meet Sergeant Kennedy again and to give a better account of myself than I did last time.

Again, I am so very sorry, Alexandra, for every-

thing. Hurting you has been my biggest regret. I'll do everything I can to make amends.
Yours,
Annabelle

Alex read through the letter three times, confused by its contents and their meaning. How was she supposed to interpret this? Annabelle wanted to be friends? Annabelle loved her all those years ago? Could she really be friends with Annabelle?

Something in her felt strange about it. She had loved Annabelle and been hurt so deeply by her. She wasn't sure that was something she could just move on from? Could she?

"Ma'am, an absolute honor to meet you. I'm Julia Wilding." Alex stood to shake Julia's hand and studied her for a second. Julia wore a pantsuit and heels, and her hair and makeup were perfectly done. From a distance, she could have passed for mid-thirties, the same age as Alex. On closer inspection, Alex saw the tiny lines around Julia's eyes and mouth, and re-categorised her at closer to fifty. Julia's dark, shiny hair was in a glamorous updo. Her skin was smooth and brown. She oozed power, efficiency and intellect from every pore. Alex immediately had a good feeling about her. Alex had told her father's office that she wanted a strong, confident, intelligent woman as her advisor. It looked like they had delivered that in spades.

"Julia, my pleasure. Thank you for coming to meet with me today. Please, do call me Alexandra. Take a seat."

"Alexandra. Thank you." Julia sat across the table on the terrace, opposite Alex. It was a warm day with a light breeze. Alex always enjoyed spending time outside, if and when she could. Alex wore a casual dress in a pistachio green, with heels. She liked the way she felt in this dress. It was a new one and she had loved the colour straight away.

Dresses were something Alex wore because she loved them. Her style was actually not something that had been cultivated for her as Princess Alexandra, but was rather something she had cultivated herself. She loved dresses in all the different colors and fabrics that she could find. She loved high heels and how they made her feel. It was all too easy to feel tiny. She was small and her body was delicately made, but Alex loved how feminine she felt in a dress, and also how powerful she felt when she wore heels.

Alex always had her hair and makeup done whenever she was meeting anyone or leaving the house. Alicia was super efficient at it now because she had been working for Alex for so long. Alicia could have her looking good in less than half an hour, for just an everyday sort of look. Alex felt confident in her look today. She liked it. She wanted to show her best version of herself to Julia Wilding, while all the time assessing her.

Jess bustled in through the door with pots of tea on a tray.

"Julia, Jess will bring us a light lunch. I was thinking a chicken caesar salad. It is one of my favorites. Would you like the same, or would you would like something different? Please just let Jess know."

"I'll have a nicoise salad, please, Jess."

Jess nodded, "Of course, Ms. Wilding. Anything else?"

"That will be fine. Thank you." Julia smiled kindly at Jess. Alex liked how Julia addressed Jess by her name, and she also liked how Julia hadn't been afraid to order for herself. So many people went along with whatever Alex decided. So many people were intimidated by just being around her.

"So, Julia, please tell me a bit about yourself and why you want to work with me."

Alex put the ball right in Julia's court.

"Well, I have actually been working as personal assistant to Deborah Carmichael for the past ten years."

Alex nodded. She had known this bit already. Deborah Carmichael was a high-ranking politician and someone that Alex respected. It was a good choice for Alex to take on someone well versed in politics.

"Now that Deborah is stepping down from politics, I am looking for my next venture. It is important for me to work only for people who are aligned with what I believe in, and frankly, I'm struggling to find another politician whom I respect in the way I respect Deborah. I actually approached the palace to enquire about working with you months ago when you came out publicly. It was a big move, and something I have an immense respect for. It would have been <u>so</u> easy for you not to. So easy for you to have married the Swedish prince and sat prettily at the top of your castle, keeping your desires behind closed doors."

Alex smiled. "For a long time, I thought the same. It actually took my meeting Erin and seeing her belief in me, that made me realize there was another way."

"You are a brave woman, Alexandra—and that, I can get on board with. I never thought I would see the day we had an out lesbian princess in the British royal family."

"Do you mind my asking about your personal life?" Alex sensed a kindred spirit in Julia.

"Of course. If there is any future hope of us working together, I am happy to be an open book. We will need to have an open dynamic between us, to enable me to work to the best of my ability for you. I am gay, Alexandra. Absolutely. I have been out since I was twenty years old—forced out before I was ready at the time perhaps, but I have no regrets. I had a long-term partner, Helen. We were together for twenty years, but I lost her to cancer five years ago."

"Oh god, Julia, I am so sorry. I cannot imagine the pain you went through." Alex jumped with the shock of it.

"It was the worst pain that there is, Alexandra. Helen was the kindest, most lovely soul. She made me laugh every day. I adored her. Having Helen taken away so young and watching her fade in front of me was the most painful thing. It was quick, really. There were six months from her diagnosis to her death. I guess that was some kindness, that Helen didn't battle helplessly with it for years, but nothing quite prepares you for that level of loss. She was forty-two years old. No age at all."

"I'm sure you know, Julia, but I nearly lost Erin a few weeks ago. Under very different circumstances, but the fear of life without her was all encompassing. I am so very sorry for your loss. Helen sounds like the most beautiful person."

"She was. I was so very lucky to have lived my life alongside someone like her. I feel grateful to have had a great love. It is something that not everyone gets to experience. I guess I do regret that we never had children. That is always something I kind of wanted, but my career was a big focus for me and when Deborah's political star rose, I became absorbed in that, and the years slipped away."

"You think you will date again?" Alex felt Julia's pain acutely. Now that she knew what it was to be so in love with someone, the thought of such a loss was huge to her.

"Oh, Alexandra," Julia laughed. "You still have

the optimism of youth. I think it very unlikely that I will have another romantic attachment. It isn't a priority for me. I had my great love. Of course, I wish I had had her longer, but I would rather have had what we had, than not at all. You have your great love now, Alexandra. My career is my focus now. I would love to work for you. I can guarantee you that nobody would work harder for you. My political knowledge would be of great advantage to you and I can study hard in the king's office for the next few years, to gain a true understanding of both the role and the Crown."

Alex felt enamoured by Julia. Not in a romantic way, of course, but because Julia wanted to commit to working with her, and in the way that Julia had devoted her entire life so far to a brilliant politician whom Alex admired. Also in the way that Julia was the right kind of person, one whom Alex genuinely wanted alongside her.

Alex stood and Julia reacted quickly and stood too. Alex outstretched her hand.

"Julia, I absolutely want you on board. I know you are the kind of person I want on my team and it would be an honor to have you."

Julia took Alex's hand in her own warm one and gripped it firmly.

"Alexandra, thank you so much. I assure you that I will not let you down. I will be by your side for the future, Ma'am. You are exactly the monarch that this country, and in fact the world, needs right now."

"Perfect. You will start in the king's office to shadow and learn. Meanwhile, we will meet every week on Wednesday, at least in the beginning, and more often when required."

Jess arrived with their lunch and they both sat to enjoy it. The thought of Annabelle's letter still lurked in the back of Alex's mind, but she chose to leave it there for the time being.

4

A couple of weeks later, on a Wednesday at lunchtime, Erin and Vic bowled into the castle following Erin's first ride back. They had decided that Erin's recovery was going well. She still felt pain in her ribs, but it wasn't nearly as debilitating as it had been. She had had an easy ride on Shimmer that morning and felt so alive. Erin felt like everything would be okay again.

Alex had approached her a couple of weeks back with the letter from Annabelle. Erin had recognised the confusion on Alex's lovely face. What was she supposed to do about it? She wanted Erin to decide, but Erin knew she couldn't tell her what to do in this case. That wasn't what happened in a healthy relationship.

"Lex, you have to choose what to do here, but I absolutely will support you one hundred percent in whatever you choose. If you want her in your life as a friend, I am right here with you and I will make every effort to get along with her. You are under no obligation, though. You don't owe Annabelle anything. You just need to choose what is right for you."

Erin didn't feel threatened by Annabelle. Sure, she was beautiful, sexy, and very wealthy. But nothing could threaten what Erin had with Alex. Things were so strong between them, and Erin was sure there was nothing that Lady Annabelle Delacourt could do or say that would change that.

"Almost fucking forgot how to ride, haven't you? All this time you have been milking being a patient. Anyone would think you got shot saving the princess's life or something." Vic was ribbing her as usual. Erin punched her on the arm.

"For fuck's sake, bodyguard. You are fucking strong. We both know that. You can't go round punching people with that kind of super-freak strength."

As they ran into the lounge, laughing and

smelling like horses, they spotted Alex in conversation with a glamorous woman with shiny dark hair and expensive-looking shoes. They both turned to look at Erin and Vic, who suddenly felt like naughty children who had been caught misbehaving.

"Oh fuck, sorry about my language," Vic blurted out, oblivious to the fact she had just said *fuck* as part of her apology.

"Alex, so sorry." Erin composed herself quickly, apologizing for Vic's slip and their interruption. "I didn't realise you were meeting in here."

Alex smiled and ran over to Erin jumping to hug her, reaching up to kiss her face. Alex looked effortlessly perfect in a light yellow dress that floated when she moved. Erin felt that familiar rush flood through her, as Alex threw herself at her.

"No need to apologize, ladies. We are done with the work stuff and were just having a chat."

Alex looked across at the dark-haired woman. Erin couldn't help noticing how attractive the woman was. "Julia, this is my gorgeous partner, Erin Kennedy, and my good friend, Victoria Grey-Hughes." Alex was holding Erin's hand now as she turned to Erin and Vic, "This is Julia Wilding, my new and most excellent advisor."

Erin smiled and offered her hand to Julia. "A pleasure to meet you, Julia. I have heard a lot about you."

"And I, you, Sergeant Kennedy."

"Erin, please."

"Of course, Erin." Julia smiled, and her smile was warm and genuine. Erin liked her right away. Julia offered her hand to Vic, who seemed to be stunned into silence. *I wonder what's up with Vic?* Erin thought. "Victoria," Julia continued, "lovely to meet you. Please don't worry about your language earlier. I actually found it very funny."

Vic muttered something and couldn't look at Julia. Erin was confused, but then distracted by Alex's hand in her own.

"Anyway," said Alex, "Vic and Erin, you should both go and shower. My father is visiting and would like to see you both." Alex looked at the big grandfather clock in the corner of the room. "You've got about forty minutes. He will see us in the Grand Hall and lunch will be served."

"Jesus, Alex. You could have warned me!"

"This *is* your warning! It is a last minute thing. I

promise I didn't know until just now. Now go get a shower; you smell like a stable!"

Erin grabbed Vic's arm and dragged her off upstairs.

"What on earth is going on with you, Vic?!"

"Oh fuck, Bodyguard. Did you see that woman, Julia, the princess's new advisor? Isn't she like *super* fucking hot? She is like the most stunning woman I have ever seen."

Erin laughed loudly. She wasn't expecting that. "Victoria Grey-Hughes! That is the first time I have seen you swooning over a woman. Now pull yourself together and get in that shower. The bloody king is going to be here soon!"

"I don't care about the fucking king. I only care about Swoony-Julia. Swoolia. I'm going to marry Swoolia. That's it. For sure. One day, I will marry Swoolia."

"You definitely said last week that you were only going to marry Idris Elba. Now it is Swoony-Julia?"

"Hmm, excellent point. I think I like Swoolia even more than Idris Elba. Perhaps he has been relegated to second position in the Swoon Olympics." Vic looked thoughtful.

"Well, there isn't time for Swoon Olympics

now, so *get in the shower!*" Erin thrust a towel at her, laughing and pushed her toward the guest room she usually used. It was practically Vic's own room; she stayed so often.

Erin rushed to shower, change, and get Vic looking presentable. She knew Vic had grown up knowing the king, so it wasn't as much of a big deal to her. However, it was a big deal to Erin—not only was he Alex's father, but he was also the king of their country. It was definitely a big deal every time she saw him.

She dragged Vic back downstairs under strict instructions to stop swooning and being weird around Julia.

They made it to the Grand Hall just in time—at least, before the king arrived.

Nothing with the king was ever low-key. Erin wondered if royal meetings would still be such a performance when Alex became queen. It was already complicated going anywhere with Alex, but the king was surrounded by so much more security and ceremony. Fifteen people entered the Grand Hall with King George. Some were security, some were his assistants, and god knows who the others were.

He moved straight to the head of the huge

table, while his entourage scattered toward the shadows at the sides of the massive room.

Julia, Alex, Vic, and Erin moved to the other set places at the dinner table.

"Thank you for being here." The king's voice was loud and commanding. Erin found it hard to distance her future father-in-law from the man she had seen on television so often her whole life. When she first met Alex, Erin had found her to be different from the public princess, but the king looked and sounded exactly the same in person as he did on television.

"I have called this dinner to make an important and special announcement." He fixed Erin with his gaze. His eyes were blue like Alex's, and it seemed strange seeing Alex's eyes in his big, meaty face. He was a large, overweight man and bore no other resemblance to his daughter.

"Sergeant Kennedy. First, I would like to thank you for saving the life of my only daughter and the future monarch of our country. I will be forever in your debt. Alexandra is vital to the future of this country and your dedication to keeping her safe is something millions of people are very grateful for. To honor your outstanding courage and heroism, I will be awarding you with the George Cross. It is the highest honor and medal I can award a civilian for outstanding bravery at great personal risk, and I think it is hugely fitting for what you have done."

Erin felt tears begin to bead in her eyes. A bravery award from the king? Could life get any more surreal? She felt Alex's hand squeeze her thigh under the table and Alex smiled at her.

"Well done, my darling," she smiled. "You absolutely deserve this."

Vic started cheering and whooped loudly. "Well done, Bodyguard! Great work!" She had managed to say a whole sentence without swearing for once, and Erin couldn't decide if it was the king or Swoony-Julia that Vic was trying to impress. Most likely, it was Julia. Vic was probably the only person on the planet who thought that crushes trumped kings.

"Well done, Erin. Honestly, I saw the footage on television. You were so very brave jumping in front of the princess. It showed dedication and love above and beyond." Julia smiled across the table at Erin.

"Thank you, Your Majesty," Erin said to the king. "And thank you so very much, everyone, for your kind words. I am overwhelmed. It was my absolute honor to risk my life for Alexandra and I would do it again in a heartbeat."

The King coughed loudly then cleared his throat.

"There will be an awards ceremony organized and you will be officially presented and honored. You should invite your family and whomever you like. I will have details sent to you."

He coughed again. "Someone bring me a whiskey. Scotch. Ice. Large," he shouted loudly and to nobody in particular, knowing that his command would be attended to quickly and efficiently. He was the king after all. "And serve the food sooner rather than later. I'm hungry."

5

Alex was dealing with her mail a few days later. She had finally decided to write back to Annabelle.

Dear Annabelle,

I am so very sorry to hear about the troubles with your marriage. I completely understand how we are conditioned, and have been since we were very young, to internalize heterosexuality and indeed to gravitate toward certain men who fit within our social status as heterosexual partners.

It was hard, and it took me many years to find a way to be brave enough to come out myself. To live authentically. Honestly, I needed Erin to bring that out in me. Erin Kennedy is an incredible woman, whom I absolutely adore.

I am willing to forgive, Annabelle, and move forward with a friendship. Many years ago, I did love you very much. Your leaving devastated me. However, I found a way to heal from that loss and to get over you.

Perhaps this doesn't need saying, but I would nevertheless like to make it clear: there will never be a romantic future between us. It is Erin whom I love and will marry.

In pursuing a friendship with you, that understanding needs to be crystal clear. I did love you years ago. But before our love, we did have a great friendship, and I believe we can get back to that.

So, in short, I accept your apology and we should absolutely catch up sometime. I would love for you to meet and get to know Erin.

Fondest regards,
Alexandra

Alex filed the letter, ready for Jess to mail, and picked up a short letter that had arrived from her mother. She had already read it multiple times, but she did so again.

. . .

Alexandra,

I cannot stress strongly enough that you should not go forward with this wedding. It isn't a real wedding, marrying another woman. I don't know what you are thinking. You cannot marry in a church because it would be a sin before God. Do you really think that this country wants the monarchy to split from the Church? It doesn't. God doesn't want that.

Do the right thing for once in your life and come to your senses. Do not go through with this farce.

Kind regards,

Your mother, Cecilia.

Just as she was staring sadly at the letter, Julia arrived. Alex was pleased to see her.

"Thank you for coming on such late notice, Julia. There is something I wanted your advice about. After a discussion with my father, we have decided to move forward with our wedding. We would like to get it planned and for it to take place within the next couple of months. The issue we have is that of the Church. I think that we need to look at splitting the monarchy from the Church. I do not want to marry in a church, and I don't see any way that I can become head of the Church of England after my father if I didn't marry in a church."

"I have no hatred of religion, but I also have no personal loyalty to it. I don't see it supporting same-sex relationships, and therefore I cannot see myself representing such an institution. How can I tell children that it is okay to be gay, and then support an institution that says the opposite?"

"I entirely agree, Alexandra. I think we need to look at pursuing a split from the Church. I don't think the split would need to happen before your wedding, but it would need to take place at some point—ideally before your father dies, assuming he is in agreement. Where would you like to marry?"

"Honestly, if it could be anywhere, I would want it to be here. This castle is my home. I love it, and I know Erin does too. The gardens and grounds are beautiful. We could organize it here. What do you think?"

"You know what, Alexandra? You can have anything you want. It is your wedding! Let me meet with with your father and his office to plan for your nuptuals, and also for the split from the

Church. I can have your wedding up and running pretty quickly if you like. If you don't want a religious service, I know a great non-religious celebrant who could perform the marriage, if you want."

"Oh, yes that would be wonderful! Please go ahead with all of that. Also, I got this letter from my mother." Alex handed the letter to Julia with a sick feeling in the pit of her stomach.

Julia read it quickly and then smiled sadly at Alex.

"Would you like a hug?" Julia opened her arms.

Alex folded gratefully into them. She hadn't known how much she really did want a hug.

"Alexandra," Julia started as she held Alex and rocked her in her arms, "Your mother is wrong. Completely wrong. Your relationship is valid, your love is real, and your wedding will be perfect. You are making the right decisions and I am right here with you. There will always be people who cannot open their minds to a same-sex relationship, so they will never understand it. Unfortunately for you, your mother is one of those people. But look at the support you have around you. Look at the family you have around you that isn't even blood-related. Your mother is wrong and she is the one who is missing out, due to her own bigotry."

Alex felt mothered by Julia in a way that she hadn't known she needed. She realised in that moment that taking on Julia had been much bigger than just getting a new advisor. Julia had quickly become an integral part of Alex's team.

Alex released herself from the hug.

"Thank you," she said contemplatively. "I needed to hear that."

"No problem. I've got your back; I promise you that. I will make this wedding happen. Don't worry about the Church, or your mother, or anything. Don't let anything ruin the happiness that you and Erin have."

Alex spent the afternoon visiting a school as part of the work of Rainbows. As usual, she loved seeing the impact she could have on children.

Later that evening, Alex folded into bed with Erin. The bedroom was dark and quiet. Erin seemed stronger by the day. Getting back into riding was doing her recovery a world of good.

"I replied to Annabelle. I wrote that I forgive her and that we can be friends."

"Great. I can't wait to meet her properly when she isn't trying to steal my woman," Erin said lazily, as Alex found her space—nestled in under Erin's arm with her right leg and arm flung across Erin. She liked being naked with Erin and feeling Erin's hot skin smooth against her own.

"I'm not going to reply to my mother's letter. Julia is going to field it for me. Are you happy to have the wedding here, honestly?"

"Of course! This place is incredible. Who wouldn't want to get married here? Alex, I would marry you anywhere; you know that. What's important on the day will be me and you. It will be easy to get lost in the occasion of it all, you know? There will be hundreds of people there and television cameras as well. But let's not forget that underneath it all, it's just us. Me and you."

"Thanks." Alex snuggled in tighter to Erin. It felt like everything would be okay if Erin held her tight enough.

"Oh, I meant to tell you the other day, but there were kings and awards and stuff and I got sidelined and forgot...Did you know that Vic has a massive raging crush on Julia?"

Alex laughed. "What?! No way?! Is that why she was acting so weird?"

"Yes. Totally weird. She has re-named her Swoony-Julia or Swoolia."

"Oh my god, you have got to be joking! She is going to have to keep that under wraps in front of Julia."

"I mean, Julia is totally hot though. Like older, classy femme hot."

Alex punched her. "Oh my god, you are crushing on Julia too?!"

"I mean, she's no Princess Alexandra, but she is pretty hot. You think Vic has a shot?"

"No way! I have to work with Julia. It is important, and Julia is...well, yeah, classy and very beautiful and Vic is.... well, she's just Vic, isn't she? She's completely mad, she swears *way* too much and she's basically a mess."

Erin laughed. "Vic is mad, yes. Well, that's up to you, to tell her to keep her hands off Swoony-Julia. I'm not getting involved. You can 'Princess-Command' her to stay away."

"Oh, god, I might have to. Julia is a vitally important royal advisor, not just some piece of ass for Vic to swoon over."

Erin laughed and Alex snuggled into her more

deeply. She felt her lips so close to Erin's skin and she kissed the side of Erin's breast lightly. Alex felt Erin's whole body react to the touch of her lips.

God, she loved their connection.

It took barely anything beyond a simple touch to electrify their passion.

She moved her lips to Erin's nipple and sucked at it, alternating harder suckling with light nibbles with her teeth. Alex pulled Erin's quickly erect nipple into her mouth. Erin moaned and her body moved as though begging Alex for more. Alex felt like she needed Erin so badly, like she needed to forget her day and her worries in Erin's body.

She moved automatically down Erin's body, seeking space between Erin's legs, her mouth seeking out what it so desperately needed and wanted.

She took Erin's folds into her mouth, alternately suckling and licking, taking whatever she could in her mouth in an almost infantile need to taste Erin and to feel her in her mouth. She knew it was more about her own pleasure than Erin's, but Erin didn't seem to object. Alex felt like she was making out with Erin's pussy as though it was her mouth—kissing it deeply, pushing her tongue inside, and burying herself in the scent, the taste, and the wetness of it.

Erin responded and Alex loved the sweet sound of her moans, coupled with the sweet taste of her. Erin's hips moved involuntarily to push herself more into Alex's mouth. It was as if she wanted to be entirely in Alex's mouth. Alex opened her mouth wide and pushed her tongue deep inside Erin. She kissed and sucked more and more, and found herself getting off on the experience of fucking Erin like this. This was all about what she was getting out of it.

"Turn around," Erin murmured and Alex understood what she was suggesting—sixty-nine position. She knew that with her face buried between Erin's legs, she would orgasm within seconds on Erin's face. Erin clearly knew it too.

Alex spun around lightly. "Are you sure you are okay with me on top? Don't let me hurt you." Erin responded by pulling Alex down onto her. She had pillows under her head, which helped with the height discrepancy. Alex felt herself face down again between Erin's legs, relaxing back into the licking and sucking and kissing she so enjoyed. She was engulfed bye the scent and the taste of Erin. Feeling the pressure of Erin's mouth against her own sex was enough to tip her over the edge. She came loudly and hard with a mouthful of Erin. Her orgasm plunged right through her body and she felt the release she had craved so badly rush through her as she collapsed completely onto Erin, with her face still between Erin's legs.

"Lex, can you get your fingers in me from that angle? Keep your mouth on me, I want to come."

Alex shook herself back to life and found a way from her position to angle her hand round and push her fingers into Erin and up towards her G spot. She focused her mouth on Erin's clit, suddenly thinking about Erin's pleasure. She got an instant response, feeling Erin move and groan beneath her. Erin was still licking Alex and Alex liked how it felt. She felt her own orgasm building again alongside Erin's. She felt Erin tighten around her fingers and Erin's body tensing beneath her, and she chose that very second to grind herself down on Erin's face and take another orgasm of her own, simultaneously with Erin's. She came hard on Erin's face, feeling Erin orgasm beneath her.

She had had so much great sex with Erin, but this was one of those where she felt so truly connected with her.

She slowly and carefully turned herself back around, being careful not to hurt Erin's ribs. She noticed her own wetness all over Erin's face, neck, and collarbone and she went to work—gently running her tongue over Erin's face, her lips, her neck, her collarbone.

Erin moaned lightly with pleasure and held her close, kissing the top of her head. Alex felt like the luckiest woman in the world.

I am so absolutely in love with this woman.

6

The presentation ceremony for Erin's George Cross medal was to be held at the palace in London. It was a huge event with many people invited by the king. Because of the nature of Erin's act of bravery in saving Princess Alexandra's life, King George intended to celebrate Erin's award above and beyond any other recipients of the honor.

This ceremony and following party were all planned in honor of Sergeant Kennedy, for showing extreme courage and for risking her own life in order to save Princess Alexandra. It was going to be filmed and shown live on television.

Part of Erin was overwhelmed by all the attention, yet at the same time, she knew it was just the start of the rest of her life. Her life was in the public eye now. Soon after this, there would be the royal wedding, and then there would be the rest of their lives together. There would be constant media attention, watching everything they did, and Erin knew she needed to get used to that.

Erin and Alex dressed for the event in clothes chosen by Natalie, Alex's stylist. As usual, Alicia was on hand, doing their hair and makeup.

Erin was dressed and ready, and sitting with Vic—both of them waiting for Alex's makeup to be done. Erin looked over to see that Alex was dazzling as usual in a long sky-blue, sequined dress. The light bounced off of every sequin and Alex seemed to light up the room. Her silvery blonde hair was curled and pinned up, with loose tendrils around her face. There was a comb pinned into Alex's hair, encrusted with diamonds and sapphires. She also wore a beautiful diamond and sapphire necklace. The stones were huge and matched the couple's engagement rings. The stones shimmered in the light. Erin cringed for a second, thinking how much they were worth. Being royalty was a different world, where hugely valuable jewelry was everywhere. But Alex looked incredible. She always did. Every inch the princess. Every inch what the people wanted to see.

Vic was wearing a long black dress and Alicia had done her hair and makeup as well. She really did look striking. However, Erin looked around to see Vic, kneeling on the floor in her dress, playing with a now fully-grown Audrey.

"Vic, you will be covered in dog hair," Erin warned. "You look really great, but I'm not sure that dog hair is going to add to the look. Audrey's hair is the worst when you are wearing black."

Vic laughed and rolled on her back, play wrestling with Audrey. There was really no hope.

"Will Swoolia be there tonight?" Vic called from beneath the gangly Great Dane. "Oh fuck, she's drooled on me. Alicia, will you tidy me up before we go?"

"*Julia* will be there tonight," Alex interjected, "and under absolutely no circumstances will you call her Swoolia or behave weirdly."

"Should have guessed, Princess Fun Police is out. Can I call her Swoony-Julia instead? Audrey! Arghhh." Audrey was licking Vic's face with enthusiasm.

"Vic. Seriously. I need you to remember that I am Princess Alexandra and Julia Wilding is a vitally important royal advisor. I need you to behave! I need you to not call her Swoolia!"

Vic didn't respond, but just laughed and extracted herself from underneath Audrey, who was still trying to lick her.

Vic had been spending a lot of time at the castle since Erin's accident, and Alex had offered to have her own horses moved over to the royal stables. So one way or another, Vic had practically moved in. At times, it was hard to believe someone like Vic had had the dedication necessary to win an Olympic medal, but the one time she was able to switch on and focus was when she was riding and training the horses. Vic's complete inability to hold down any kind of relationship had helped her, because now horses were everything to her. She was a naturally gifted and brave rider, but her years of dedication had helped her reach the top. It was almost as if, having achieved what she had by the age of thirty, Vic had chilled out over the past few years. Like she didn't have the same drive as she once did. She had been there and had gotten the t-shirt—or in her case, an Olympic gold medal—and she was enjoying new challenges. Training young horses and helping to train Erin seemed to be her new passions.

Alicia finished with Alex, and Alex stood up.

God, she is stunning. Erin never failed to be blown away by Alex's beauty.

"You look incredible, Lex."

"Not bad, Princess, not bad," Vic chimed in.

Alicia turned to see Vic and nearly fell over in shock. "Victoria! Oh my god! I leave you for a second and look at the state of you. Come here!" Alicia went right to work with her lint roller, trying to roll the dog hair from Vic's black dress. Audrey had fallen asleep and was snoring in the corner, oblivious to the havoc she had caused. "Is this . . . dog drool? Oh my god." Alicia had wet wipes on the go and worked like crazy to remedy Vic's appearance.

"Come the fuck on, Alicia, I need to look my best if Swoolia is going to be there tonight."

"Do *not* call her that!" Alex commanded in her most authoritative princess voice, the one that had most people jumping to obey her. Most people, but not Vic, who was laughing at her.

"Swoolia... *Swooooolia*...S*woooo*—"

Just then, there was a knock on the door and Sergeant Joanne Davis's voice called out, "Ma'am, ready to leave when you are."

Erin knew damn well that the cars, the drivers,

and the security would have been ready to leave for the past half hour. Joanne's knock on the door was a polite way of saying, *Hurry up! We will be late.*

"Thank you, Joanne," Alex answered.

When the Range Rover pulled up outside the palace, select members of the press were there. They had received permission to photograph guests on arrival.

Alex and Erin had traveled in a separate vehicle from Vic. As they got out, the familiar craziness ensued. Erin knew that they were the guests of honor on this occasion, but that was the same for every occasion. Everywhere they went, people wanted to photograph them. That was the magnetism Princess Alexandra possessed, so people around the world craved pictures of the spectacle she created, just by existing. They wanted to know everything about her. They wanted photos of her every time she left her home.

They especially wanted photos of Erin and Alex together. They wanted to know everything about the couple, including what they each were wearing and who the designers were. Today, Erin felt comfortable and confident in a dark, sapphire-blue pant suit that had been carefully designed to match Alex's jewelry and complement her sky-blue shimmery sequin dress. Erin knew they looked incredible together.

Alex had briefed her about the poses they would strike for the photographers. She knew they would want to see the rings, so the two women had run through some poses before they left home. Positions that showed off the rings, as well as their connection.

Erin's left arm draped loosely around Alex's shoulder—far enough around that the gemstones on her left hand glinted against Alex's collarbone, right next to Alex's huge diamond and sapphire necklace. Alex's left hand reached up to meet her own. Their poses looked casual, but in reality, they were anything but.

Erin was getting used to putting on the big beaming smile that the photographers wanted to see, as well as creating intimate poses with Alex that shone with love. It wasn't hard for Erin to express her love for Alex. The tough bit was doing it while knowing that photographers—and the therefore the world—were watching every moment.

They made it into the palace, finally escaping the flashbulbs.

Prince Nicolas was there and he rushed up to Erin as soon as he saw her. He gripped her hand firmly and smiled warmly at her. His brown eyes were open and trusting. "Erin, huge congratulations on this award. Nobody could have done more. You are a hero."

"Thank you so much." Erin smiled at Nicolas. "It was just instinct, I guess, along with years of training. Thank you so much for looking after Alex when she needed care the most—when I was in surgery. She said she would have broken without you and Vic. You have been such a great friend to her, and indeed to us both. So I thank you for your kindness."

"You are so very welcome, Sergeant Kennedy. If there is ever anything I can do, you know you have a friend in me. Now go and enjoy your evening. This is all for you, you know." He waved his hand around the ballroom. There had been no luxury spared. The finest decor, food, and drink were on display. In addition, a collection of royalty and other important people were there to witness Erin's award ceremony.

It felt crazy to her. Most people's girlfriends

weren't at risk of assassination, but if they ever were, Erin reasoned, it would only be natural to want to protect them.

She sometimes wondered about the wisdom of her decision to throw herself in front of flying bullets. Perhaps it said something about her. Contrary to what a lot of people thought, throwing yourself in front of bullets wasn't high up in bodyguard training school. It was generally thought that everything you should have done had gone to shit, if you were at a point of having to take a bullet to save the life of the VIP.

The security team should have definitely checked the venue more thoroughly. There is no way that anybody should have made it in there with a gun. Mistakes made on that day that had nearly cost Erin her life.

This was her first semi-public engagement since the incident. She wondered if she would feel fear or anxiety the next time she was at a public engagement. She hoped not.

Erin had trained hard, so she would always act to protect. There wasn't really any room within that mindset for fear. Having said that, Erin didn't know what she was worrying about. She would never work as a bodyguard again. She would never need to work as anything again. But, on some subconscious level, Erin was always protecting Alex. Was that a work and training thing? Or was it just the kind of person Erin was, that she had a fierce drive within her to always protect her princess?

Erin didn't know the answers to any of those questions.

"Darling!" Erin knew the voice straight away as she turned around. "We are *so* proud. Just *so* proud. Aren't we, Alastair?" Erin's mother enveloped her in an overbearing hug and a cloud of sickly sweet perfume. Her parents had visited her in the hospital and Erin supposed she should be grateful that she had a family, and that they cared about her and supported her. Mostly at least. She just couldn't be close to her parents in any way.

"Alexandra." Erin's mum swept Alex up, almost off her feet, and Alex graciously let her.

"Gina," Alex responded, every inch the Princess. "So lovely to see you both here today. Thank you for attending. It is a wonderful day to be proud of Erin and what she did for me on that day."

"Oh, Alexandra. Why, yes, of course. Also, we are *so* delighted to hear about your engagement.

Oh, do let me see your ring. So beautiful. Goodness, what a beautiful stone."

Erin stopped listening to the babble and engaged in polite small talk with her father. She always appreciated when Alex took on her mum, when they had to see her parents. Alex was socially brilliant and her mother was absolutely charmed by her. Erin's mother loved everything about Princess Alexandra and had read every article the press had ever printed about her. Erin's mother particularly liked how femme Alex was, in a way that Erin had never been. She relished every opportunity to discuss dresses, shoes and makeup with Alex.

The next hour passed by in a blur, with so many people congratulating Erin and thanking her for saving the princess's life.

Erin was surprised, but not overly so, when Lady Annabelle Delacourt swept in with freshly highlighted hair surrounding her face in a big mane. She wore a sleek and classy gold-coloured dress that matched the golden highlights in her hair.

"Sergeant Kennedy. Huge congratulations on your award. I would like to apologise to you for what happened last time we met. I am very sorry for how I must have come across. I would like to do what I can to give you a better impression of myself. It is indeed an honor to be here tonight." She turned toward the princess. "Alexandra. So lovely to see you. Again, I am so very sorry. I was so grateful to receive your letter."

Erin was skeptical, but decided to give Annabelle the benefit of the doubt. "Thank you, Lady Delacourt."

"Annabelle, please."

"Annabelle. Thank you for your kind words. Your apology is accepted. We all make mistakes. You are a long-time friend of Alex's and I am keen to get to know you better. Please, call me Erin."

"Erin, of course." Annabelle reached across and kissed Erin's cheek. Her perfume was strong and sensual. Her kiss and the way she lightly touched Erin's cheek was in no way inappropriate, but it almost felt like it was. Annabelle was the kind of woman who oozed sex appeal from every pore. There was nothing overly sexy about the dress she was wearing, but her body was all long lean legs and bold curves. The way she moved, like liquid silk, was sexual. The way her eyes and her mouth moved made it seem as though she were inches away from initiating sex at any given moment. Annabelle's voice dripped with heat.

Erin could see how easy it would have been for the young Princess Alexandra, already confused about her sexuality, to have become absolutely entranced by this woman.

But Alex was much more together now than last time she had seen Annabelle.

"Annabelle, thank you so much for coming. It is lovely to see you." Alex stood on tiptoes in her heels to kiss Annabelle's cheek. "So lovely to have you finally meet Erin properly. We would love for you to visit the castle sometime. I'm sure we could arrange a tennis match. We have Victoria Grey-Hughes staying with us at the moment too."

Annabelle laughed heartily and her big breasts bounced. "Ah, Victoria. She used to be a great tennis player and a fierce competitor. I would love to come and play with you all at some point. Erin, how is your tennis?" Annabelle looked at Erin.

"Getting better!" Erin said. "Alex is training me up. Bit of a setback lately, what with getting shot and everything."

Annabelle roared with laughter. Her green eyes glinted mischievously. "I cannot wait to visit and play! I also hear you have been making waves in the eventing world, Erin. Lovely horse you have. Have you managed to get back to riding?"

"Yeah, I'm just taking it steady after the shooting, but I am recovering well. Shimmer is incredible. I am very lucky to have such an amazing horse. All thanks to Alex."

Alex snuck her arm around Erin and looked up at her lovingly. "You deserve all of the best things, my darling."

Erin reached down and kissed her. She felt the familiar rush through her body that always came with kissing and touching Alex.

Annabelle smiled at them. "Huge congratulations on your engagement. It is lovely to see Alexandra so happy and in love."

Alex's hand moved to Erin's ass and sat innocently on her hip as Annabelle smiled at them both. What kind of weird powers did this woman have that made the most innocent things seem sexual?

"Attention, everyone." The king's voice boomed from the stage at the front of the room.

Silence swept through the room. In the same way that Alex could command silence immediately, her father held the same power.

"I would like to thank you all for attending the

ceremony this evening. We are here to honor a great and courageous woman. This woman has saved the life of my daughter and your future queen, Princess Alexandra. Sergeant Erin Kennedy threw her body into a shooter's line of fire, literally sacrificing herself for the princess. There could be no greater act of heroism. Sergeant Kennedy underwent lifesaving surgery to repair the damage done by the bullet, and we are all so very grateful that she survived and is recovering well. The George Cross is to be awarded for acts of the greatest heroism, or for most conspicuous courage in circumstances of extreme danger. I am in no doubt that Sergeant Kennedy's actions on the day when there was an attempt on my daughter's life fit this criteria in the highest way possible. I would like to hereby present the George Cross Medal to Sergeant Erin Kennedy."

The room started to cheer and all eyes moved to Erin. Erin felt Alex's hand in her back. "Go on. You have to go up there."

Erin moved up to the stage to be presented with the medal from the king himself. A dark blue ribbon with a silver cross attached to it was pinned onto Erin's jacket. Bulbs flashed everywhere as photographers went mad.

Erin couldn't quite believe her life now.

7

Alex woke early the following morning and went out for a walk with Audrey on the castle grounds, while the grass was still wet with dew. She couldn't believe how grown up Audrey was now. She was taller than Alex when she stood on her back legs.

She got back to the castle and prepared Audrey's food, leaving her to eat and run around outside while she headed back up to their main living quarters.

She had been so proud of Erin last night. Her partner was an absolute hero and now had the medal to prove it.

As she headed back along the upstairs corridor, Alex passed Vic's room. She heard the unmistakable moaning of sex noises from behind Vic's door.

Alex's eyes widened and she bolted back to her own bedroom, finding a just-waking Erin. "Oh my god! You will *never* guess what." Erin looked bemused and Alex didn't give her time to answer.

"Vic is having sex!"

"What?! Who with?! How do you know?!"

"I just heard them. Through the door."

"Are you sure it was sex?" Erin looked confused.

"Of course it was sex! I know what sex sounds like!" Alex responded adamantly. "Who can it be with?"

"Did it sound like a man or a woman?"

"Oh god, I have no idea."

"Maybe it was Swoolia."

"It had 100 percent better *not* be Julia! It can't be Julia. Julia is definitely not the kind of woman who would have casual sex with Vic."

Alex took a deep breath. "Anyway. I can't think any more about Vic having sex."

There was a knock on the door. Erin shrugged a robe on.

"Come in," Alex called.

It was Jess, pushing a trolley. "I have celebratory breakfast for you, Sergeant Kennedy. The princess ordered it for you. We have all sorts of things on this trolley. Whatever you would like. Huge congratulations on your medal. We are all very proud of you."

"Thanks, Jess," Erin smiled. "Maybe we can take it on the terrace. It looks like a nice day." Erin and Alex's main living room was on the first floor, next to their bedroom. The castle was so big that most of the time, they just lived in one section of it. The living area had huge french doors that opened out onto a roof terrace. Often, when the weather was nice and they had the time, Erin and Alex enjoyed spending the first hours of their morning relaxing on the roof terrace, and taking coffee or breakfast there.

"Of course," Jess said, and wheeled the breakfast trolley out onto the terrace.

"I'm going to jump into the shower quickly, then I will join you for breakfast, Future Mrs. Kennedy. Thank you for ordering breakfast. I hope there are avocados in there because I'm really in the mood for avocado and egg on toast." Erin smiled, shrugging off her robe and kissing Alex. Alex still hadn't gotten used to how attracted she was to Erin. Erin, naked, looked like some kind of sportswear model. Her body was finely muscled and strong, and her abdominals were sharply defined.

God, she's so hot.

Alex knew that Erin's body was the result of the hours she had spent in the gym they had downstairs, along with a lifetime of fine-tuning her body. That level of dedication, in itself, was so attractive. Alex felt her eyes sweeping over the naked lines of Erin's body, as Erin turned and headed to the shower. The scar on the back of her ribcage from the bullet wound and the resulting surgery was very evident, but it didn't do anything to detract from her body. Alex admired how the dip of her lower back splayed out into a strong, round ass, and she smiled to herself before heading out to the terrace to plate up some avocado and eggs on toast for Erin.

She added some bacon on the side because she knew Erin loved bacon.

Alex poured herself a coffee and helped herself to some fruit salad and Greek yogurt, which she always enjoyed in the morning. There was something about a fresh selection of fruit that Alex loved.

She sat quietly in the early morning sunshine

for a couple of minutes before Erin came over and joined her, delighted to see her breakfast.

Seconds later, Vic bowled out through the big french doors, squinting at the daylight. She wore red tennis shorts and a loose fitting pink T-shirt. They didn't match at all.

"I thought I smelled food. Great news. I am fucking starving." Vic headed to the trolley and started helping herself. Luckily, Jess had planned ahead for this eventuality and had told the chefs prepare plenty of food. Vic took a piece of toast and stacked it up with sausage, egg, bacon and a large quantity of tomato sauce—followed by another piece of toast on top. She sat down and took a massive bite, sighing in satisfaction.

"Worked up an appetite, have you?" Alex asked her, drily.

Vic didn't respond, and Alex wasn't sure she had understood her teasing. Before she could ask more, another figure swept gracefully through the french doors, wearing a red silk kimono that Alex knew for a fact was her own, which Vic had borrowed weeks ago and had never given back.

Alex looked at Erin and caught her conspiratorial smirk. They could barely stop themselves from laughing! Alex chose to play dumb.

"Annabelle. Lovely to see you again, and so soon!"

"Alexandra, Erin, thank you for letting me stay. Victoria assured me that you wouldn't mind. You see, unfortunately my driver had a flat tire, so I was unable to make it home last night. Victoria very kindly offered to let me stay here." Annabelle was as smooth as ever.

Alex could still hear the loud moaning that she had heard through the door earlier, and she couldn't stop trying to decide which one of them it had been.

"She is very kind, Victoria is." Erin almost laughed. Alex had to stop looking at her or she knew they would both dissolve into laughter. Vic was totally absorbed in her sandwich.

"Please, help yourself to food and drink, Annabelle." Alex indicated the trolley. It was funny how her feelings around Annabelle had completely changed all of a sudden. She could see how beautiful Annabelle still looked in the morning light, and how her breasts were bursting out of the kimono that was too small for her. But Alex realised in that second that she didn't crave Annabelle anymore. What they had was so long ago that it seemed like another time. Alex had grown up so much since then and so many things had changed.

Annabelle helped herself to some coffee and lit a cigarette. Alex smiled to herself. Nothing had changed. That was the behavior of the Annabelle from years ago, living off nicotine, caffeine and red wine.

Vic finished her sandwich and went right back for another one. Alex marvelled at the sheer amount of food that Vic could eat, and yet still look lean and wiry. It was all the riding Vic did each day. She was always riding, or on her feet coaching riders. Alex was also fairly sure that Vic still couldn't cook, which was why she was always so excited by life at the castle, where amazing food was consistently produced by skilled chefs—as if by magic. Vic would devour it, as though eating her last meal.

"Erin. This is a little awkward," began Annabelle, "but I am asking you because you are closest to me in size. My driver is coming to collect me, but I have only last night's dress—which I obviously cannot put on to go home. Are you able to loan me some casual wear? Maybe jeans and a shirt?" Annabelle fixed Erin with her most charming look.

"Um, of course, Annabelle. Come with me and I'll see what I can find."

Annabelle was right. She might have been a different build than Erin, but they were both tall and bigger in size than either Alex or Vic.

As soon as they disappeared, Alex confronted Vic.

"So, Victoria, care to enlighten me about any developments in your sex life?" She knew Vic couldn't keep a secret.

Vic sighed deeply. "Ugh, I'm so hungover, Princess.... I'm not sure I can talk about it."

"Come on, Victoria. We all know you can't keep anything to yourself."

"Oh, okay, *fine*. I had sex with Annabelle Delacourt *all* night long. We did *all* the sex in *all* the ways, and I am fucking exhausted now! I need her to go home so I can get some sleep."

Alex couldn't help laughing. "Thank you for keeping away from Julia. I do appreciate that. You can sleep with Annabelle as much as you like."

"Ugh, I wasn't going to tell you. I thought it might be weird. Didn't you two have a thing that summer after you finished college?"

"How on earth do you know about that? Nobody knows about that."

"Gotcha! I mean I didn't know for sure, but I do now. I just remember you being, well, very close. And since I now know that you are a massive lesbian, I put two and two together and . . . well . . . here we are. Is it weird?"

Alex took a deep breath. "Oh, god. No, not weird. I really thought nobody knew about me and Annabelle. I was devastated when she left to marry Rupert. Honestly, Vic, you can help yourself. It was very over between us, a very long time ago."

"Oh god, I'm not sure what I want. I mean she's crazy. Annabelle is nuts!"

Alex laughed. "You are nuts too, Vic!"

Vic laughed too. "Well, I know that, but I'm not sure there is room for us *both* to be that way! Plus she has a husband, and all those fucking children and well, you know."

"They are getting divorced, I think." Alex took a big sip of her coffee, which was cooling nicely.

"Yeah, she did say that. But, anyway, it isn't really a relationship. I think it was just a one-time deal. I think Annabelle was using me for my body and for her own sexual gratification. She was *wild* sexually. She ate me alive. I'm not sure I will ever fucking recover."

Alex remembered why she enjoyed Vic so

much as a friend. Vic was totally hilarious. "Such a hardship to be used for your body by a beautiful and sexually open woman."

"Ugh... I'm not sure I can ride today. I think I need to go lie down and recover. Will you tell the stable girls I'm off sick, and they can give my horses the day off? Just put them in the field for the day. They would love a day off enjoying the grass and the sunshine."

"Okay, Horse Girl. You go have a rest and I will let the stable girls know. I will also see Annabelle out, as I'm assuming you have too much morning-after shame to actually have an adult conversation with the grown woman you spent the night with."

"You would assume right."

Alex relaxed in the sunshine and picked up a newspaper to peruse the photos of herself and Erin from the night before.

She winced with excitement. Their rings matched perfectly with her necklace, and also with their outfits.

Ah, we look SO good together!

~

That afternoon, Erin was out riding Shimmer while Alex met with Natalie, Alex's stylist, as well as the famous fashion designer, Madeleine Boujard, to discuss and plan their wedding outfits. Madeleine was a glamorous French woman with impeccable Parisian style. She must have been over sixty years old, but barely looked a day over forty-five. Alex had often worn Madeleine's designs and had never doubted that she would have Madeleine design her wedding dress.

"So, *ma petite*, tell me what you are thinking?" Madeleine had always called Alex *ma petite*. It meant *my little one* and Alex enjoyed the term of endearment. So many people got hung up on calling her *Ma'am* or *Your Majesty*, and while it was indeed the correct way to address her, Alex liked people who weren't afraid to mix it up.

"Well, obviously white, but I am thinking lace. We need to stay conservative, but we also need 'magical princess.'"

"*Ma petite*, I have some exquisite, light, chantilly lace. Here, let me show you." Madeleine's assistant went over to the clothing rails they had brought with them and produced a roll of beautiful white lace. Alex fell in love with it right away.

"Take off your dress and step onto the step,"

Madeleine commanded, indicating the wooden block she always had Alex stand on for fittings. Alex slipped her dress off over her head. She had worn simple white underwear and a strapless bra so Madeleine could do her work.

"Oh, I love that lace. It is so delicate. It will be perfect on you," Natalie said, admiring the fabric.

Madeleine worked quickly, her nimble, tanned fingers pinning lace and white silk around Alex's body.

For so many in high society, dress fittings were a necessary evil, but Alex adored them. She was fascinated by the process. She loved the different looks that could be created quickly with pins and fabric. She admired the incredible talent of the designers and also of her stylist. They could make things happen with fabric.

They tried many different adjustments, and two hours later Alex looked in the mirror and knew it was finally right. The skirt was full and had a train. But nothing too big because Alex was petite, and a massive skirt would drown her. The dress was backless. The shoulders and long sleeves were made of the light, delicate lace, which rested on Alex's skin. It was sexy, yet conservative, yet still "fairytale princess"—all at the same time.

Natalie met Alex's gaze and smiled knowingly. She knew Alex and her taste so well at this stage, that no words needed to pass between them.

Madeleine stood back with her arms folded, and admired her handiwork.

"*Ma petite*, we are ready."

And they were, Alex knew for sure. She had to pinch herself to believe it. This was her wedding dress for her own royal wedding. She was going to marry Sergeant Erin Kennedy and she couldn't wait.

8

The weeks moved on and Erin found herself lost in a world of wedding preparations. It had all been done for them and Alex was a professional decision maker, but Erin still found herself dragged into decisions like which cake tasted best and which flowers looked nicest. She went along with whichever choice Alex made.

None of this mattered to her. All that mattered was the smile on Alex's lovely face when she was happy. All that mattered to Erin was the two of them, and not the big circus of the royal wedding that had begun around them. Erin wished it could always be about just the two of them and not about the whole world, but she didn't have much choice in that. Their lives were public property, and the weight of that became increasingly clear to Erin.

They couldn't go to normal places, like normal people. Their only real privacy was here at home, or on the grounds of the castle. Sure, there were staff and security everywhere, but they left the couple alone as much as possible when they were at home.

Erin couldn't say that she didn't enjoy her new life of absolute privacy, but the costs associated with it took some getting used to.

Erin had returned from taking Audrey out on her morning walk around the grounds, and had left the big dog munching enthusiastically on her breakfast. Erin wandered into the lounge area to see Alex still in her silk lounge pants and delicate silk top. It was an outfit that Erin had always loved on Alex. Her natural morning look, before her hair and makeup were done. Alex's nipples were always prominent under the silk. This morning, she was sitting and going through her mail, looking troubled.

Erin wandered over and leaned down to kiss the top of Alex's ashy blonde hair. It smelled fresh and of Alex's shampoo, which was one of Erin's favourite scents. It spoke of "Home Alex," before she had been layered in fragrance and made up to become "Princess Alexandra."

"What's up?" Erin asked, taking a seat next to Alex.

"Oh, god, it's another letter from my mother telling me not to split the monarchy from the Church, and not to marry a woman. There have been a few other letters with various versions of the same thing. I've been ignoring them. I haven't responded. Julia has responded on my behalf and Cecilia has been advised to back down on this, but it hasn't stopped her. She is still going."

"You still care what she thinks, don't you?"

"I *wish* I didn't. I really wish I didn't. Even though she has never really been a mother to me and handed me off to nannies as soon as I was born. My mother is the least maternal woman ever. There is just this thing, this invisible tie that binds me to her, and I wish that it didn't. I wish that I didn't care. Like I say I don't care and I try to convince myself of that, but she's still there, and she's my mum and ... well .... I don't know. It's not like I am going to change my plans to please her. But I just hate this. All of this." Alex's lovely face had a troubled frown.

"You could ask Jess to filter out mail from her?

To forward it to Julia and have her go through it instead?"

"Hmmm, it might be a good idea. I don't know how much more of this I can read." Alex sighed deeply. "Anyway, enough of that. What are your riding plans today?"

"Well, I'm feeling so much better. I know I have missed out on the National Championships, but there will always be next year. Today will be my first day back to jumping. Vic thinks I am ready. I feel ready. Vic has been jumping Shimmer, so Shimmer is fit and well for it. I can't wait, really! It feels like I have been waiting for so long."

Alex smiled, and her smile was like sunshine itself. "I'm happy for you. I hope it goes well today. How is your scar feeling lately? I forget about it sometimes. You seem so much like yourself again now."

"Ah, it feels good, honestly. I am aware of it because the scar tissue feels tight, I guess. It's hard to explain. It isn't pain anymore, but like a tightness around my ribs where the scarring is. As if it needs to learn to move again. I'm thinking of getting help from a physical therapist to try and get movement back."

"Of course! Good idea. I can have Julia organise

someone for you, if you like . . ." Alex was always offering her staff to assist Erin. Erin still found it tough to get used to having people do things for her, but she knew she needed to start accepting the help that came with her new position.

"Sounds like a great plan. I don't have anyone in mind. I mean, I'm sure I could still access support from the police's medical department, but it might be better having someone visit me here."

"Yes, definitely. I'll have Julia organize it with one of our doctors." Alex took Erin's hand and smiled. She liked being able to fix things. Alex was so used to the world of having staff. Although she was down-to-earth for a princess, she still was a princess.

Annabelle arrived a couple of hours later, after they had showered, dressed, and finished breakfast. Annabelle had been coming over to play tennis with Alex on mornings when Alex didn't have other commitments. Alex had been enjoying the games and rebuilding a friendship with Annabelle. Erin had been entirely supportive of it —she never wanted to be controlling over whom

Alex spent her time with. But she couldn't help but feel a nagging concern somewhere deep inside her whenever Annabelle was around. She couldn't quite put her finger on it. Annabelle had been lovely and kind, and consistently charming since she had been back on the scene. She had been going out with Vic, who seemed to have gotten past her initial reservations and now seemed happy with how things were going. Their "relationship" hadn't been labelled that. They were both keeping it casual. Vic was still flighty as hell and Annabelle was in the early stages of a divorce.

Erin wished she could be happy for them, and for Alex and her renewed friendship with Annabelle. But deep down inside, Erin just didn't trust Annabelle and she couldn't shake that feeling.

Annabelle looked striking in a short, white tennis dress that showed off her long, tanned legs. Erin couldn't keep her eyes from straying for a moment over Annabelle's body. It was just typical Annabelle; she always dressed to be admired. Alex was happy to see her. They chatted, then headed out to the tennis courts.

Erin headed down to the stables to meet Vic. Vic liked to start her mornings early and get her own horses exercised before she coached Erin and Shimmer.

The weather was sunny with a light breeze, and Erin enjoyed walking down to the stables. Everything seemed fresh and possible again. Audrey ran over from the direction of the tennis courts, delighted to see her. Erin smiled and leaned down to run her hand over Audrey's massive head. "Hey girl, how's the tennis going?" Audrey nuzzled her big head into Erin in response, then walked along next to her, toward the stables.

Shimmer was in her stall. She had been groomed by the stable girls and was now a gleaming, dazzling white. Erin knew it was a constant battle to keep white horses white. She knew the girls would have been in there early with a bucket of warm water and shampoo, spot-cleaning any stains Shimmer had picked up overnight.

It didn't bother Erin if Shimmer didn't look immaculate every day, but she knew it was the stable girls' job, and their pride, to have the royal horses looking perfect at all times.

She went via the feed room, and grabbed a couple of carrots for Shimmer. Shimmer took them appreciatively and nuzzled her hand for more. Shimmer's muzzle felt like pure velvet and again, Erin felt so lucky to have her.

Just as she was enjoying a quiet moment with her beautiful horse, hooves clattered into the yard and Vic arrived on her sweaty-looking bay horse, Romeo. Romeo was big and handsome, and Vic loved him. He was still young and had a bright future ahead of him. Vic jumped off him athletically and landed on her feet. She walked over to Erin.

Sarah, the stable girl, came rushing out of the tack room to grab Romeo.

"Thanks, Sarah. Just give him a washdown, please, and make sure he gets out in the field for some grass this afternoon. He will be fucking hungry; he has just had to work hard."

Sarah automatically took Romeo and headed off to the shower area. The stable yard was kitted out with the best of everything. They had a big wash box with hot showers available for the horses, and then hot lights that turned on to dry the horses. The horses generally loved getting their showers and then relaxing under the warm lights as they dried. Erin wished that they had had such a good set up as this when she had worked with horses before, but she was grateful for it now.

There was always more than enough staff, too, so the horses were never rushed. The girls had enough time to provide the absolute best care for each horse.

It was a novelty that Erin could definitely get used to. So many horse yards were over-horsed and understaffed. So many horse yards couldn't (or didn't) want to pay for the staff they really needed, so they ended up with stable girls having to cut corners in order to get through all the work they had to do in a day.

"I thought we could have a bit of a chat about your plans before we head out," Vic said to Erin, as she stood outside Shimmer's stable.

"Sure. Shall we go and sit by the field in the sunshine?"

They headed over to the bench where they could watch the horses in the field, wandering around and munching the grass—enjoying the feel of the sun on their backs and the ability to just be horses, as naturally as they could.

It was rare that Vic was ever serious, but she was very capable of being so, particularly when it came to the horses and competitions. Those were her real passions in life.

"So, looking at what we have coming up . . .

you've obviously missed out on the national championships because of getting fucking shot. Inconvenient, sure, but my honest opinion is that you'll be a much better rider in another year's time. So it may not be a bad thing. You'll give a better account of yourself next year. I think we aim to get you and Shimmer to the national championships next year, and also to one big international competition. By then, you should have a realistic chance of performing well—of winning or at least placing highly. I know this is not something we have discussed yet, but the following year is the Olympics. The British team selectors will be watching riders carefully next season. I think, if you continue to improve as you have been doing, that they will look at you. If you can achieve a high placing in one of the big competitions, they will have to consider you for a place on the British olympic team."

Erin felt her own eyes widening. Sure, she had dreamt of the Olympics all those years ago. Sure, it was what she had worked toward. And now she had a horse that was good enough, a coach that was good enough, and all the financial and physical support she could dream of. Of course, it would still take work and luck, but Vic was right to bring it up. She was right in that it was a possibility. The thought of it felt huge, though. Something Erin had barely considered.

"Wow, I mean, you are right in your theory, but it just seems like such a big dream and like, well . . . . So many things could go wrong."

"Bodyguard," Vic sighed. "There will always be things that can go wrong, but we shouldn't let that stop us from fucking dreaming. The Olympics has been my dream since I was old enough to ride a pony and first saw the Olympics on television. I knew it was the biggest and the best. I knew it was going to be my life's work.

I got to the Olympics eventually, and I didn't go there to give a half-hearted performance. I was lucky. I had an incredible horse. And although my family situation is a bit fucked, I was born into a wealthy family who had stables, fields, and horses. I had practically everything I needed. I just needed the dream, the dedication and the passion to make it happen. You can fucking do it. You just need to believe in yourself a bit and commit to this over the next couple of years. Shimmer is entirely the kind of horse that is capable of it. She is entirely the kind of horse that will make the British team selectors' eyes light up."

Erin thought for a minute, then she asked a question that had been troubling her for some time.

"Why did you let Alex buy Shimmer for me? Why didn't you take her for yourself? You knew how good she was. You had already been training her with her last rider."

"Oh, Bodyguard, that question been on your mind for some time? You should have just fucking asked me! I did it already. I went to the Olympics. I won the medal. I had the horse of a lifetime. Some people make their national team and it is all they want to do for the rest of forever. They want to keep doing it, to stay at top level and keep on winning. Keep on wearing that Union Jack flag."

"But honestly, being on the British team was a lonely time for me. Ironically, I didn't feel like I was good enough. I never felt like I fit in. I got constant critique from the team manager and they wanted too much input in how I trained my horses. They wanted me to change my coach. I had to shut up and take it long enough to get selected for the Olympics, because that was what I really wanted."

"But when I finally got there, I felt lonely and sad every night in my hotel room. I felt the most miserable I ever have. I just said to myself, *you perform for these three days of competition, you get the best out of this incredible horse, and you can live the rest of your life as a champion.* So that is what I did. I quit the British team as soon as we got home. It was no fucking life for me. Obviously, I still love the horses. I love training young horses and riders like you. Shimmer is a superstar. She deserves a rider who is hungry enough to take her to the top. That's you, Bodyguard. That isn't me anymore. I like the young horses, the difficult and challenging horses. I like to take the horses that people don't believe in and prove them wrong. That is what I enjoy these days."

"God, I had no idea. I'm sorry it was so shitty for you. Well, thank you for Shimmer. I *am* hungry, you know. It just didn't turn out so well, last time I was hungry. Horses are full of risk. Accidents happen. There is so much that could go wrong. But I won't let it stop me. I am going for it, you know. I'm excited to get back to training properly now that I'm feeling so much better."

"Thank fuck for that. I don't want to be coaching a quitter!"

Erin laughed. Vic could only be serious for so long.

"So, how is it all going with you and Annabelle?" Erin asked, conspiratorially.

"Oh my fucking god, I have no idea. I mean, good, I think. The sex is *insane*. But I don't really do relationships or commitment. It just isn't for me." Vic screwed her face up.

"Well, I mean, you could do commitment now . . . now that you aren't solely focused on Olympics and horses and everything, right?"

"I mean, that makes sense and everything, but it's like, how do I change the habit of a lifetime?"

"Have you met her kids?"

"Fuck, no."

"They will want to start calling you *Daddy*," Erin teased.

Vic punched her. "I'll push you off this bench and shove horse shit in your face if you carry on. I am not joking!"

Erin wasn't really sure how serious Vic was, so she decided to back off a bit.

"Do you trust her? Annabelle?" Erin couldn't help herself asking.

"Absolutely not! But then, I don't trust anyone, so maybe that doesn't mean anything."

"What about Swoony-Julia? Any progress there?"

"Ah, Swoolia, the love of my life. I am still, definitely, one-hundred percent going to marry Swoolia—but your fucking princess is definitely trying to keep us apart. Anyway, <u>you</u> are the one getting married. Are you wearing a dress?"

"No, thank god! Natalie is working alongside the French designer woman to design me a smart pantsuit that will compliment Alex's dress. God knows what that actually means. There is talk of a lace cravat and I don't know how I feel about that, but I do trust Natalie and Alicia, at least. Honestly, they have made me look better than I ever have. I see these photos of me with Alex in the newspapers, and I don't even recognise myself. Now <u>there</u> are two women who are exceptionally good at their jobs."

"To be fair, you've got that right. They even managed to make <u>me</u> look good for your big posh palace awards night, and *that* was some achievement."

Erin laughed. She loved her friendship with Vic. She loved having her living at the castle, but she was no closer to nailing her concerns about Annabelle.

What was it that made her so uneasy around the woman?

9

lex met with Julia, and the plans for separating the monarchy from the Church were put into place.

Nothing would happen until after the wedding. People would undoubtedly speculate about the separation, given that the royal wedding wouldn't be in a church, as was tradition. But Julia said it wouldn't matter.

It was better to give the people a wedding to celebrate, and then start to make changes to the monarchy afterward.

Alex had been spending a lot of time with Annabelle, and she had found herself enjoying her rekindled friendship. Annabelle had been nothing but kind and lovely, and hugely supportive of the wedding.

Alex wasn't sure what was really going on between Annabelle and Vic. It seemed like Annabelle was spending the night more and more often. Alex had heard them having sex more times than she had wanted to—and Vic hadn't held back the details. It felt weird sometimes, hearing about Annabelle's sex life with someone else.

All those years ago, when she'd had Annabelle in her bed, when she had feasted on Annabelle's body without really having a clue about what she was doing, Alex had just wanted to love her.

Alex told Vic that it was fine now, for her to be seeing Annabelle, and it <u>was</u> fine. Alex didn't want to be with her. It was totally fine. But somewhere underneath all the "fine," it felt a bit weird. Alex could still remember being obsessed with Annabelle's body. Whatever Annabelle wore, her body always seemed to be on display—either the long legs, the round ass, the big boobs, or all of the above. It was hard to look at her and not see it.

Alex felt she was pretty far past Annabelle now. She hoped that Annabelle would be good for Vic. Although in public, they seemed like nothing more than friends—and perhaps barely even that.

Their entire relationship seemed to take place behind Vic's bedroom door.

Erin had planned a surprise date that Alex was excited about. It was a lovely, sunny, late-summer afternoon and time was drawing closer and closer to the date of their wedding. Alex waited outside the back door of the castle, as she had been instructed. Erin had been in the gym, but she arrived on time, freshly showered. Looking totally hot in short, sporty shorts and a tight t-shirt that Erin knew was exactly the kind of outfit that drove Alex wild. All Alex could see was her long, muscular legs and her biceps, bulging from the short sleeves of the shirt. She could see the outline of Erin's small breasts under the thin fabric of the t-shirt, and the tempting shape of her nipples. Erin's hair was still wet and was slicked back behind her ears. It was cut shorter now and it was beautifully dark against her tanned skin, contrasting with her green eyes that shone brilliantly in the sunshine. Alex had never seen her looking so attractive.

Erin smiled lazily while the sunlight caressed her face.

"Good afternoon, Princess Alexandra. You look very beautiful in your sundress. I have a plan for you this afternoon. First, I'll need you to wear this blindfold while I take you to the location." Erin produced a black, silk blindfold that Alex knew damn well was from their bedroom collection. She smiled knowingly and presented herself for Erin to blindfold.

She felt the blindfold being placed over her eyes and the band of it fitting snugly round the back of her head. Everything went black and her hearing felt super-aware all of a sudden. It felt electric when Erin firmly took her hand.

"Follow my lead," Erin said, her voice like liquid chocolate.

Alex found herself walking silently, following the hand that was guiding her. In itself, the level of trust required to walk without her sight was a lot. It didn't feel like a time for conversation.

Alex had no idea which direction they were going in. The grounds of the castle were extensive. She started off trying to guess where they were going, but she just confused herself so she decided to relax her overthinking mind and just to go with the experience.

Alex felt the changing of surfaces under her feet—from the sponginess of grass to what felt hard and not totally even, like a track or a path of some kind. Then she felt twigs and leaves crackle under her feet. That meant they were near trees, although there were a lot of wooded areas in the big grounds of the castle. Then, as they walked further, she heard running water. They must be next to the stream that ran through the castle grounds. It ran through one big section of woodland in particular.

The sound of the water got louder. It was the waterfall, for sure. There was a waterfall in the woodland on the hill.

"Here, careful. I'm going to lift you up." Erin's voice reassured Alex that she knew where she was. The waterfall was about thirty feet high. Next to the waterfall there were big rocks that had been positioned to enable a relatively easy climb.

Alex felt Erin's hands from behind on her waist, lifting her up as though she was as light as a feather. Lifting Alex had always been easy for Erin's strong arms. Alex felt weightless, then she felt herself faced with a rock, which she climbed onto.

"Okay, just wait there a second while I climb up." The process of Erin boosting Alex up then climbing up herself was repeated three more times as they progressed higher up the waterfall. Alex could hear the water rushing, and every time she liked feeling Erin's hands on her body. She remembered playing in the waterfall as a child. She remembered playing on the rocks and climbing up them, but she hadn't been in this spot for years.

As they got to the top, Erin led her away from the edge and pulled off the blindfold.

The forest was beautiful and the sunlight danced its way through the gaps in the trees. Alex felt it on her skin. The waterfall was as beautiful as it ever had been, but Alex felt a new-found appreciation after having been blindfolded. After hearing it first, before seeing it.

She looked around and she saw that a little picnic had been set up. There were blankets on the forest floor, and what Alex recognized as a big catering box from the kitchens on a low table off to the side, that was no doubt full of food and drink for them. Alex felt herself smiling. It was the most beautiful scene she could imagine. She loved the way the light fell on Erin's face, which was full of hope.

"Thank you so much! This looks amazing." Alex saw that they were totally enclosed by the trees on one side and the waterfall on the other. It was a private area, where they were actually alone.

"I thought we could spend some time just enjoying the day here first, and then move on to the picnic in a while." Alex caught Erin's gaze and saw the look of desire in her eyes. It rushed through Alex's body. She knew what Erin was suggesting and she suddenly found her own body hugely responsive.

"I think I would enjoy that." Alex smiled her best seductive smile.

Erin took her hand again and led her to some blankets on the woodland floor, right next to where the stream ran past. Alex thought they would sit down, but instead, she found that Erin was lifting her up again. Erin's hands were firmly under her ass and Alex felt her legs move naturally to hold onto Erin around her waist.

Erin moved so that Alex's back was against a tree. Alex could feel the rough bark against her back. She felt lust slide right through her as she was pinned tightly between Erin's body and the tree. She wrapped her legs tighter around Erin's waist and her breathing started to quicken. She could smell the fresh and slightly masculine sporty scent from Erin's shower gel.

Erin kissed her deeply and Alex felt it everywhere. She felt Erin's tongue pushing into her mouth. Erin's hands were now under her dress, which was up around Alex's waist. Erin's hands were gripping her ass tightly. She felt Erin pulling at the thin fabric of her underwear and her clit throbbed as the underwear tightened against her pussy.

Fuck, how is it even possible to get this turned on for someone this fast?

Alex couldn't think of anything else, except suddenly wanting Erin inside her so badly. She needed to feel Erin deep inside her. Nothing else mattered until she felt that.

Suddenly Erin pulled hard on her underwear and it strained for a couple of seconds, biting into her hip, before Erin jerked it again hard and it ripped. Erin had ripped her underwear right off her. Alex felt the warm breeze against her suddenly exposed pussy, and she liked how it felt.

Erin stopped kissing her and pulled her mouth

away. Alex marvelled for a second at how beautiful Erin's face looked in the sunlight that flickered through the leafy tree canopy. Erin's eyes were almost amber with desire in the sunshine.

"Open your mouth," Erin murmured and Alex obeyed, then immediately felt something pushing into her mouth. She smelled the sweet scent of sex and realised it was her own underwear going into her mouth. She could taste herself on them. A bolt of desire shot from the taste on her tongue to the rapidly building wetness between her legs.

She felt Erin moving something in her own shorts and slightly adjusting the way she was holding Alex up with her hand. Alex was praying that Erin was going to find a way to penetrate her. The tree bark was scratching at her back and Alex wanted it to mark her. She wanted to feel it. She wanted to feel everything. She suddenly felt something hard pushing at her pelvis, as Erin went back to the position they had been in before, with both her hands on Alex's ass.

"You need me to fuck you hard now, right?" Erin's eyes met her own.

Alex was still unable to speak, still tasting the heat of her own desire, so she nodded vigorously.

"Do you want any warm up?"

Alex shook her head confidently. She was already there. Erin could get her there mentally, so she was so very ready for it. She was desperate to feel Erin inside her.

Erin nodded agreement as her right hand snaked further around Alex's ass and ran between her legs, slipping easily through. Alex knew she was so wet.

She felt Erin guiding something to her pussy, it could only be a dildo. Erin must have been wearing a harness under her shorts and she must have slipped the dildo into it just now. Alex felt every beautiful inch of it as it pushed into her, opening her up. She loved nothing more than the sharp feeling of it pushing deep inside her, all the way in. It was thick, and she felt her body fight to adapt to the feeling of it in her. Every nerve ending inside her was on fire.

Erin took hold of Alex's ass cheeks again and moved her slowly up and down to start meeting Erin's slow thrusts. Alex felt completely at Erin's mercy the way she loved to be, pinned between the big tree and her lover, being fucked deeply by the big dildo.

She heard her own muffled moans through the underwear that was still stuffed in her mouth.

Erin began to thrust faster, fucking her harder. Alex felt lost in it, melting into the sensation. There was nothing that satisfied her more than being taken roughly and fucked hard. She enjoyed different kinds of sex, but this was what made her feel the most alive and the most primal. Her connection with Erin was pure raw passion.

Alex could forget who she was entirely for these minutes, because all she could do was feel. She felt herself gushing repeatedly as Erin fucked her deeply. Her eyes were closed.

"Look at me." Alex felt the thrusting stop. She heard Erin's voice and opened her eyes, meeting her intense gaze.

"Can you feel my harness brushing against your clit?"

Alex focused for a second and pushed her hips forwards, nodding.

"I want you to focus on that. Position yourself so it feels good. Keep looking at me as I fuck you."

Alex felt Erin begin to fuck her again, gradually building intensity. Alex moved her own hips so her clit was rubbing against a ridge on Erin's harness. Every time Erin thrust into her, her clit moved against the harness. As things moved faster Alex could feel herself getting closer to orgasm.

"Keep your eyes open. Look at me," Erin commanded, and it took everything Alex had to maintain eye contact as her body moved toward its peak.

The tree bark was biting into her back, which just added to the sensation.

Alex focused on the position of her clit. The waves of pleasure began to build up the tension within her until they hit that point of no return. Then they crashed through her body like a crescendo. Rush after rush from deep inside her, as she kept Erin's gaze. It felt like the most vulnerable, incredible thing. She felt her body collapsing, the dildo still deep inside her, holding her up. She felt the underwear fall from her mouth.

She felt Erin carry her away from the tree and lie her down on her back on the blanket. She could still feel the dildo in her and Erin on top of her. She dissolved into a moment of post-orgasmic bliss, feeling her pussy clenching around the dildo.

Then she felt Erin slip out of her and off her and Alex lay in the warm sunshine with her eyes closed, totally spent and relaxed. Her dress was still bunched up around her stomach, but she didn't care. She liked feeling the breeze. It felt good against her sensitive pussy.

I love how she fucks me so much. She knows my body and my mind so well.

Alex snapped back to reality when she felt Erin above her again. Erin was naked and straddling Alex's right thigh. Alex could feel Erin's wetness pressing into her thigh.

"I had to take my clothes off. You soaked them all . . . even up my t-shirt!"

Alex laughed, "So sorry. My mistake! You ripped my favorite underwear off me!"

Erin ground against Alex's thigh lazily.

"Were they really your favorite?"

"No, not really." Alex sighed and tipped her head back. Erin's finely toned body looked incredible above her. "You are my favorite. You look amazing. Like something out of a magazine."

Erin ground tighter against her thigh, "Okay, stop embarrassing me. Fucking you has turned me on so much. I just want to make myself come on your thigh—if it's alright with you, Princess Alexandra?"

Alex was in no doubt about the truth of that statement. It was always the case after Erin fucked her, that she was soaking wet and so close to orgasm.

"You can use my face, if you like?" Alex smiled sweetly at her. She knew exactly how much Erin liked coming in her mouth.

Erin's eyes lit up and she didn't need asking twice. She moved up Alex's body and knelt over her face.

Alex could smell her desire and she opened her mouth to meet Erin as she lowered onto her. Alex's tongue instinctively moved to pleasure her. She loved what she could do to please Erin so much. She alternated between dipping her tongue deep inside Erin, running long trails of her tongue through Erin's wetness, circling Erin's clit and sucking it into her mouth.

It was no time at all before Erin orgasmed hard in her mouth and Alex watched Erin's beautiful body tense and then release above her. Alex smiled to herself and licked her lips as Erin fell sideways and rolled onto the blanket.

"Oh my fucking god, that was incredible. The things you do with your tongue . . . " Alex watched as Erin closed her eyes and curled up on the blanket. Alex took her in her arms. She could still smell Erin's sex on her lips.

"So, I think I have built up a picnic appetite now," Alex said enthusiastically. Erin laughed, still curled up with her eyes closed.

Alex didn't know how anything could be any more perfect.

I can't wait to marry this woman.

10

Alex was out at a school visit when it happened. The school was a distance away and Erin knew that Alex would be out all day. Vic was still at the stables. She had another rider whom she coached, and who was visiting the grounds for a lesson.

Erin had spent her morning as usual: walking Audrey, doing a gym session, and then riding Shimmer. She made her way back for lunch and a shower, and was just relaxing on the terrace when Jess burst out of the french doors, looking awkward.

"Ms Erin. There are visitors for you. I'm sorry. I couldn't stop them," she mumbled.

A few steps behind Jess was Cecilia—Alex's

mother and the current queen. Erin had met her a few times before, and Cecilia had never said more than two words to her. Erin had no idea what she was doing visiting. Behind Cecilia, flanking her, were two men. One of them, Erin knew right away: Lord Hugo. The other she recognized from photographs. It was the king's brother, Prince Arthur, who may or may not have been involved in the assassination attempt on Alex. Nothing had ever been proven and this was the first time that Erin had met him.

Erin jumped to her feet, then remembered royal protocol. She bowed her head and addressed the Queen first, then Prince Arthur.

"Your Majesty. Your Royal Highness."

She had no idea how to address Lord Hugo. If it weren't for the presence of the queen and the prince, she might have had some choice words to say to Lord Hugo.

Erin had never forgotten the way he had assaulted Alex soon after Erin had started working for her. Every single part of Erin seethed, seeing him now. She wanted to smash his smug, handsome face in.

She took a deep breath and calmed down.

Cecilia looked a lot like Alex. She was small,

poised and delicate. She was effortlessly graceful, with a face that was still strikingly beautiful, even with age. Her hair was a fine golden blonde and was pinned up exquisitely.

The difference between her and Alex was evident, though. Where Alex's face was open and lovely, the queen's face was hard. Her eyes were stern and they glinted angrily. Erin had thought this before when seeing photographs of her, but it was never more evident than it was now, seeing her here in person.

Erin knew from Alex that the queen had married for status, and had hated the king. She had had a child out of duty and had never behaved in any way that could be considered maternal towards Alex. As Alex had grown up and had become beautiful, she had taken all the attention that had once belonged to Cecilia. It had made Cecilia bitter and resentful.

The bitterness and hate had eroded her over the years. Erin knew this was what she was seeing in Cecilia.

The three of them stood on the terrace, facing Erin.

"Get out of here," Cecilia commanded a terrified-looking Jess, who knew all the details of the relationship between Alex and her mother. Erin knew that Jess would have tried to stop them from coming up, but that she would never have been able to stop the queen.

Jess looked to Erin for authorization to leav, and Erin felt a moment of love for Jess's loyalty to herself and to Alex. Erin nodded to her. Erin could fight her own battles.

"Ms. Kennedy," Cecilia said, in a voice as smooth and condescending as Erin had ever heard. Erin's rank wasn't of vital importance to her, but Erin also knew damn well that Cecilia knew her name was Sergeant Kennedy, or in fact "Erin," and that she had purposely chosen to use neither one.

"I'm not here to get into any kind of discussion. What I have to say are orders that are to be obeyed. I am commanding you, as your queen. I trust that you, particularly as a member of our royalty protection team, would want to do what is best for king and country." Cecilia spoke calmly and quietly, but with dangerous undertones.

"You will leave Alexandra. You will stop playing at this pathetic lesbian thing with my daughter. You are making a mockery of the monarchy."

"I won't leave her. I love her," Erin responded boldly. "Alexandra can make her own choices in life."

"Ugh," Cecilia made a noise that emphasized her disgust.

"And you, Ms. Kennedy, are an altogether bad choice." Prince Arthur spoke now. His voice was slightly feminine, but similarly threatening. "Alexandra's poor life choices make her a bad option as future monarch of this country." Arthur looked a lot like a younger thinner version of the king. He had the same meaty features, but a leaner version of them.

"I command you to leave my daughter. I selected Lord Hugo for her when they were both children. There could be no better partner for her for the future. If you care about Alexandra like you profess to, you will end your association with her. There is still time for her to redeem herself and marry Hugo. Aside from the fact that only a man can have a valid marriage with a woman, Lord Hugo is from very wealthy, entirely suitable—and noble—blood. And *you* are anything but. You won't even be able to *consummate* your 'marriage.' You won't even be able to give her children. What use do you think you can be to her when she becomes queen, if you can't even give her children?"

"I won't leave," Erin continued.

Cecilia nodded to Prince Arthur. He lifted a suitcase that he was carrying and flicked it open on the table. It was filled with cash. Fifty-pound notes. Bundles of them. More than Erin had ever seen or imagined.

"One million pounds," Arthur said seriously. "It's yours, upon the agreement that you will never see the princess again."

"Take your money and get out of my home. I make your daughter happy, Ma'am. I do everything to make your daughter happy, and I plan to spend the rest of my life doing just that. Alexandra will make an exceptional queen."

There was a knock on the big glass door and everyone turned to look. It was James Marshall, who was head of residential security on the castle. He was a big, muscular, intimidating guy. Erin had known him when she worked as a bodyguard, and had always gotten along well with him. She often stopped for a chat with him when she saw him on the castle grounds.

"Everything okay here, Sergeant Kennedy?"

His eyes met Erin's and she knew he had come to help her. Jess had probably gone to get him.

"The Queen, Prince Arthur, and Lord Hugo were just leaving. Maybe you could escort them out?" Erin didn't know where she found the confidence to be so assertive, given the combined power of the three people standing opposite her, but she did. She had no idea if it would work or not, and the three of them looked shocked to hear it from her. But leave, they did. Arthur clicked the briefcase shut, realizing their plan wasn't going to work. The three of them turned to follow James through the lounge area and out toward the hallway.

Erin stayed on the terrace, breathing the fresh air in deeply. She felt her heart racing.

What on earth just happened?

Later that evening, a tired Alex came home and Erin told her everything. Alex just hugged her and promised everything would be okay. But nothing felt okay at all. Alex seemed suddenly childlike, and intimidated by the power of her mother. They collapsed into bed together. With Alex's body hot against her own in the dark, and Alex not wanting to talk, they slipped naturally into sex. Erin could always get a response physically from Alex, even if mentally she was closed down. Alex moved and writhed and moaned beneath her, and as much as she enjoyed fucking Alex and giving her that release, Erin found her own orgasm completely out of reach.

"Are you okay?" Alex asked. "Is there anything I can do?"

"I just can't get there right now. I think we just need to leave it."

Alex moved up the bed and snuggled in under Erin's arm, kissing the side of her breast lightly. "I love you," she said, and Erin felt relief that the pressure to orgasm was over.

They lay with their bodies entwined together and they talked late into the night. The darkness absorbed their fears and their hopes. Alex kept saying it was fine. That it wasn't a big deal. But she hadn't been there. She hadn't seen the level of threat that they had put upon her.

Perhaps because Alex knew them all so well, she wasn't afraid of them.

But Erin knew that just because you knew the bad people, it didn't make them any less dangerous.

11

Life felt almost normal over the next few weeks. Alex spent her time doing public appearances for Rainbows, or for other royal charities, and sometimes Erin accompanied her. There was so much public support for their upcoming wedding that Alex felt overwhelmed by it. Cards and flowers were given to her constantly when she was out and about in public.

Alex wasn't afraid anymore when she made her public appearances, and she was glad about that. Everything felt calm and her security team seemed reassuringly controlled.

That nightmare day of Erin getting shot and the chaos that ensued was becoming less vivid in her mind.

Alex couldn't believe what had gone on with her mother, Arthur, and Hugo. It was absolutely unbelievable. She had thought about going to her father about it, but she hadn't done so yet. She didn't want it to seem like she couldn't manage her own problems.

Alex had discussed at length with Julia about what should be done about them. They had decided to leave the problem alone for now. The three of them had offered Erin money to leave. She had refused it. They had left. They had been no further trouble since.

Alex wondered if her mother would attend the wedding. She would have to, surely. Public perception was everything to Cecilia, and everyone would notice if she wasn't there. There was no way the king would allow her to be absent.

However, upon reflection, Alex thought that maybe she didn't actually want her mother there at all. Sometimes she thought about how much freer she would feel if her mother just died one day.

God, you can't think like that. What kind of psychopath are you?

But it was true. Her mother wasn't an everyday fixture in her life, but somehow she was always lurking there in the background, as she had done Alex's whole life. Lurking somewhat threateningly. Was the threat real or imagined? This was her mother—that had to count for something when it came down to it. How much ill could she really wish on her only daughter?

Alex didn't think she would actually do anything. Cecilia was a woman of hurtful words, rather than actions.

Alex remembered so many times in her childhood when she had desperately tried to please her mother. But nothing she had ever done had been good enough. She had been constantly disparaged and shot down, and pushed to try harder. Alex had spent time in therapy speaking to a world-renowned psychologist about it, and she knew this was the reason she had spent her whole adult life pushing herself so hard to be the perfect princess that the public wanted. Alex had spent a lifetime reaching for the highest levels of success in everything she did.

Many people would say that she had succeeded. She was the perfect princess, absolutely adored by the whole world. Alex had always looked perfect and always said all the right things.

Luckily, many years of cultivating perfection had given her a platform to be able to marry the woman she really wanted to, and to do good for the LGBTQ community.

Alex had been spending her free time at home with Erin and Audrey, enjoying the end of summer in their beautiful home.

Annabelle had been spending a lot of time there to see Vic, but also to play tennis with Alex when Alex was available. She enjoyed it, mostly. Annabelle hadn't changed and was still highly competitive. She had to win every time, which she usually did fairly easily. Alex was a decent enough tennis player. She had been coached by a top tennis coach through childhood and was a clever player, who knew the game like the back of her hand.

Annabelle was a tall, strong, powerful player who could put so much more power through the shots than Alex could. Alex could beat her sometimes, but she had learned many years ago that things were easier when she pushed Annabelle hard, but then let her win in the end. Alex had made a fine art of dropping crucial points to ensure this outcome.

Sometimes they played doubles with Erin and

Vic. Vic was also highly competitive, so they usually put her on Annabelle's team to keep fights from breaking out, although it didn't always work that way. Vic wasn't the best at tennis. She didn't quite have the skills and the speed around the court to back up her fierce desire to win.

It had been fun though, Alex pondered, having friends again and spending the summer with them. She had spent so many years alone in an isolation that she had created herself. After losing Annabelle so many years ago, Alex had been far too scared to let anyone else close. Her walls were built so high that nobody had even been allowed to see over them.

Alex was excited about today because Prince Nicolas would be arriving from Sweden to stay with them for the next week, until after the wedding.

"Nicolas! An absolute pleasure to see you!" Alex found herself throwing her arms around him and hugging him. His support and strength during the hardest times in her life had given her a deep, platonic love for him.

Nicolas hugged her back and lifted her off the floor for a second, smiling. "So good to see you, Alexandra. I am so very happy to be here." His English, as usual, was technically perfect.

Audrey was the world's worst guard dog. She wandered over and licked his hand. Nicolas rubbed her head, kindly. "You have gotten so very big since last time I saw you, Audrey Hepburn. I bet you are as tall as me if you stood upright." He looked into her eyes and stroked her gently.

"So, I hear we are having what you English call a *hen party* tomorrow night to celebrate the end of your life as an unmarried woman?"

Alex led Nicolas through the castle, toward their main living quarters. The staff had promptly moved to take his luggage for him.

"Oh, god. I mean, I really don't want to, but I have had to agree to it. Vic said it was a rite of passage, or something. I think it's a real heterosexual tradition, where a group of women wear pink and drink out of penis straws. There had better not be any penis straws."

Nicolas laughed heartily. "I have yet to experience drinking out of a penis straw. I feel honored to be invited as a man."

"I think this will be a nontraditional hen party.

For a start, Erin and I will both be there. We can't do separate ones—we don't have enough friends!"

"I always think friends are a 'quality rather than quantity' kind of thing. If they are good friends, then it doesn't matter how many there are."

Alex smiled at him. Nicolas was always so full of wisdom.

"I entirely agree. Please take a seat," she said, and indicated her lounge area. Jess came bustling through the door with an armful of mail and some flowers.

"Ma'am, Prince Nicolas," she mumbled through the flowers.

"Jess, would you please organize for us some tea, a selection of cold drinks, and some light snacks?"

"Ma'am, of course." She put the vase of flowers down on the big table, alongside many others, and put the pile of mail on Alex's desk. As usual, it had been separated into three piles. Jess moved quickly, then was out of the room and on to her next mission.

"Nicolas, I see you didn't bring a guest. Will there be anyone attending the wedding with you?"

"Ah, no. There is no one special. I've come to

realize that I already have a great and full life. I'm really not sure that a significant other of any kind is something that I need in my life. I have actually told my parents this. I think they are perhaps a little disappointed, but they have actually been very supportive."

"That's amazing! Honestly. Your parents have always been so great. I have always been a big fan of theirs, now even more so. You are lucky."

Nicolas smiled and looked at her gently. "You, not so much? I know you said in a text the other day that there were issues with your Cecilia?"

"Oh god, you cannot even imagine!" Alex found herself launching into the whole story about Cecilia's passive-aggressive letters, ending with the incident when she had approached Erin, alongside Arthur and Hugo.

"They offered her one million pounds? Where did they even get that much money?"

"My mother's family is very wealthy. I imagine they provided it? I cannot imagine that Arthur would have been able to access that amount of money without a lot of questions arising."

"Oh, Alexandra, this is difficult. What did you do?"

"Nothing, yet." Alex sighed. "What should I do?"

"The police, perhaps?"

"I don't think I can. They haven't actually done anything illegal. Immoral, yes. Very much so—but not illegal."

"I think perhaps it would be worth reporting the events—even to your own police or security, and with a level of discretion. Write down anything more that takes place. Then, if anything else happens, there will be a record."

"Julia did suggest that, actually. Oh, I haven't told you! I have a new advisor, Julia Wilding. She has come from politics and she is really great."

"Oh, wonderful news. I look forward to meeting her one day. Do consider reporting these troubling events in some way, Alexandra."

Alex was lost in thought. Nicolas and Julia were right. She should report the incident.

Jess was back with drinks and snacks. "Jess, please set up a meeting with Rob Greene, my father's head of security, along with Joanne Davis. This afternoon, ideally, when Erin is also home."

"Of course, Ma'am. I will."

Nicolas began to pour tea for them both, and Alex was yet again happy he was here.

Alex and Erin sat opposite Rob Greene and Joanne Davis.

Alex began, "I would like to report an incident, in order for there to be a record of it. However, given the highly sensitive nature of it, confidentiality and discretion is essential. I would appreciate if this doesn't go beyond those of us in this room, unless there is a necessity for it to."

"Of course, Ma'am," Rob said, and Joanne nodded her agreement.

"On August fourteenth, while I was out at a public engagement, Sergeant Kennedy was visited unannounced here at home by my mother, Prince Arthur and Lord Hugo. My mother, in no uncertain terms, commanded Erin to leave me and not to go through with the wedding. Prince Arthur had a suitcase containing what he said was one million pounds in cash, which he offered to Erin—in exchange for her not going through with the wedding. She said no. Meanwhile, my assistant Jess was concerned, so she spoke to James Marshall, our head of residential security. When he came up to check on Erin, they agreed to leave quietly. Now, I hope you can understand my concern about keeping this quiet. It is a highly sensitive situation."

Rob was a dark-haired, quiet man. He was unassuming and didn't look big or intimidating. Instead, he looked like an everyday, average guy. Alex knew from Erin that people who looked ordinary were usually the most highly skilled and capable security operatives. Their ability to blend in gave them a huge advantage in doing their job.

He sat up straight and responded. "First, Sergeant Kennedy, I am very sorry that you have had to deal with this. Both of you. I am sorry that you are meeting opposition from inside the family to your marriage. Second, looking at how we deal with it . . . I would like to take a statement and all the details from Sergeants Kennedy and Marshall, and from your assistant, Jessica Dawes. The statements will remain locked up and entirely confidential. We will not act on anything without your permission or direction, Ma'am."

"As I'm sure you are aware, there is little we can do at this time. I might suggest speaking to your father and having him speak to your mother. However, I am aware it has the potential to get complicated, so that is entirely up to you. I am very happy to discuss this with your father if you want me to."

"At this stage, I'd rather not, Rob. Thank you. I'd like you to sit on it for now. But I think that if you and Sergeant Davis have an awareness of what is going on, at least we can perhaps figure out how to manage things."

"Of course, Ma'am. Sergeant Kennedy, shall we go through what happened, and I will take a recording so I can type it up later?"

Alex watched as Erin gave her statement. Erin was calm and clear, but there it was, hanging over them—during what should have been the happiest week of their lives.

The hen party was in full swing. Vic and Annabelle had made everyone lethal cocktails that tasted misleadingly of fruit juice.

They were having the party in Erin and Alex's lounge area because there was no need for one of the big rooms for just the few of them. There was a giant, inflatable penis floating around, which Alex wasn't entirely sure was something one brought to a lesbian hen party. Nevertheless, there it was in its big pink glory. Alex was grateful she hadn't been forced to wear anything crazy, only a tiara and bride's white veil. She was also very grateful for the lack of penis straws.

There were, however, drinking games. At first, they were really fun, but Alex didn't drink very often or very much, and she was starting to feel uncomfortably drunk as the evening wore on.

Vic was desperate to go out and drive around the castle grounds in the dark to show Nicolas around. It seemed like a *really* bad idea, but Alex was in no fit state to stop them.

"I'll go with them and make sure they don't get into any trouble," Erin said. She had somehow managed to control her drinking, and she also had a much better tolerance for alcohol. She did seem like the sensible option, because Vic and Nicolas were on the floor with Audrey, laughing hysterically about something.

"I'm not going. I feel like the room is spinning. Driving around would definitely make me feel sick," Alexandra stated boldly.

"I'll stay here and look after Alexandra," Annabelle said nobly, and Alex was grateful for the company. Annabelle and Erin were certainly the most sober of the crew.

Erin kissed Alex on her way out the door and promised she would be back soon.

Alex was grateful for the sudden peace as Erin, Nicolas, and Vic left the room.

Little did she know that it was to be the calm before the storm.

12

Erin felt like the token grownup as Vic drove in the Range Rover while giggling like a child with Nicolas. It was entirely irresponsible to be driving around the estate so drunk. Erin had informed security on her way out. Now security followed in a car a distance back. Vic and Nicolas hadn't even noticed. The estate was deserted. As long as Vic could avoid driving into an immovable object like a tree, a wall, or a castle, everything should be fine.

Erin found herself constantly policing Vic. "Careful. Slow down. Mind that tree." She had sobered up pretty quickly.

Vic was getting more and more defiant and driving faster and doing handbrake turns in the wet grass. She would drive fast, then suddenly pull up the handbrake hard, and the Range Rover would spin around sharply like a fairground ride.

Nicolas loved it, and was like a child encouraging her.

Things were getting out of hand and Erin wasn't quite sure what to do. Vic was getting more confident in her ability, so she started pushing for faster and faster speeds. Erin felt so aware of how slippery the grass was.

Vic was driving down the hillside that bordered the lake.

"Careful Vic! You are so close to the lake."

"Oh, don't be such a fucking bore, Bodyguard. I'm not going to drive into the fucking lake."

She drove fast and close to the lake but not into it, and Erin was momentarily relieved.

She then spun the Range Rover round and headed directly towards the lake.

"VIC! STOP IT."

"Ooooh! Scared, are we, Bodyguard?"

As she got close, she slammed on the handbrake and the Range Rover spun around sharply. If it hadn't been for the wet grass, things probably would have been fine, but the Range Rover slipped sideways on the grass and skidded into the lake.

Nicolas and Vic laughed like children as the Range Rover bobbed for a second and then began to fill with water. They had no sense of the potential danger.

Erin went straight into professional mode and reached across to the driver's door, operating all the electric windows and opening them before too much water came in. She had made them all wear seatbelts when they set off, so she reached over and clicked each of their seatbelts, setting them free. Vic and Nicolas were still joking around.

Erin grabbed each of them, one at a time, and pushed them out the window as the car filled up. By this point, the security car had arrived and James Marshall and another member of the security team helped each of them to the shore.

"Everything okay, Sergeant Kennedy?"

"All good, thank you, James. Nobody is hurt. Can you arrange something regarding the car? I have no idea what."

They were all soaking wet and Erin figured they had ruined a very expensive Range Rover, but there was no great drama.

"Of course. I will sort that. Hey, do you need thermal blankets? We have some in the car."

"I think we are fine. It isn't so cold. A lift back to the castle might be good, though."

"Of course." James moved to talk on his radio and was obviously updating the rest of the security team about what the drunken idiots had done.

Another car arrived quickly. It had waterproof sheets across the seats, and the three of them climbed in.

"Did you fucking see that, Bodyguard? I've never seen you look so serious. Where is your sense of fun? We just fancied a little swim, didn't we, Nic?"

Erin decided there and then that drunk Vic was not someone she wanted responsibility for minding in future. She would absolutely send a member of security with Vic next time she was drunk and going out on wild escapades.

They made it back and stripped out of their wet clothes in the living room. Jess was already there with towels and robes for each of them.

"Where are Annabelle and Alex? Annabelle!" Vic called out.

"I bet Alex has gone to bed. Or possibly being sick, and Annabelle is helping her? She didn't look very good."

Vic stalked off toward Alex and Erin's bedroom

to look for them. Erin followed her, keen to check on Alex and get a shower to clean the lake off her.

As they walked into the bedroom, Erin could barely believe her eyes.

Alex and Annabelle were both naked in the bed, the covers half over them. Two dildos and a bottle of lube were on the bed next to them.

"What the fuck?" Erin muttered. She couldn't be more confused by what she was seeing.

Vic went immediately crazy. "WHAT THE FUCK? ANNABELLE!" Vic stormed over and grabbed Annabelle by the hair. "I thought you said we were exclusive?" Annabelle woke up and looked shocked to see them. She grabbed a bedsheet to cover her nudity.

"Did you two have sex?" Vic asked, looking afraid to know the answer.

"Um, yes, sort of," Annabelle said awkwardly, "I mean, just for old times' sake. Alexandra came on to me. I'm so sorry, Victoria, Erin. Alexandra just was all over me. I couldn't help it."

Erin swallowed deeply. Alex was still sleeping, oblivious to all the noise around her. Erin refused to react until she had Alex's version of events.

"Get the fuck out of my bedroom," she said to

Annabelle and Vic, her voice calm but laced with anger.

The two of them scuttled out, still arguing between themselves.

Erin took the dildos and chucked them into the shower to deal with later. She sat on the bed next to Alex and tried to wake her, shaking her shoulder gently.

"Lex, Lex baby, wake up."

Alex murmured but didn't wake.

Erin thought for a minute, trying to stay calm and rational, then she picked up the phone, calling the castle night staff. "I need a doctor please, for Princess Alexandra. I think she has had too much to drink."

It was less than half an hour before the royal doctor arrived. Jess, who lived onsite, was out of bed and bringing her upstairs.

The doctor was Emma Wallis. Emma had been working as the doctor for both the Princess and Erin ever since they had moved to the castle. She was intelligent, efficient and no nonsense. Erin got on well with her. She hooked Alex up to an intravenous solution of saline, potassium and magnesium, designed to flush out her system and free it from the alcohol.

"Please try not to worry, Sergeant Kennedy. You have done the right thing. Alexandra has had too much alcohol. I know she doesn't usually drink and she is a small person, so a lot of alcohol would hit her hard. This IV solution will sort her out and bring her around. She will be fine. I'd like to sit with you till she wakes, if that's okay? Just to be sure she is all right."

Alex woke hours later, and as Emma predicted, she was fine. The IV solution had helped her body recover quickly.

When Emma left, they were alone together.

"Lex, when we came back last night, you were naked in bed with Annabelle. She says you had sex."

"What?" Alex looked confused. "Not at all. I asked her to help me undress because I felt really drunk and then I just went to sleep. I wouldn't do that. You know that. You know me."

Erin looked into Alex's earnest blue eyes and realised what she should have already known. She did know her. Absolutely and completely. Alex would never do that.

"I know you. I know you wouldn't do that. So, basically, we have a situation. Annabelle has lied outright and she has also made sure that when Vic and I walked in, it looked like you two had sex. She was naked and there were dildos and lube out on the bed."

"Jesus. It never happened. None of it. I know I was drunk, but I would have known. I would remember something. Why on earth would she do this?"

"I honestly have no idea. I've been feeling like I didn't quite trust her for a while now, but this? She has to be trying to break us up, especially this close to the wedding. She has to be trying to stop the wedding."

A look flashed across Alex's face as she sat up in bed as though she had suddenly remembered something.

"Years ago, Annabelle was very close to my mother. I'm wondering if Cecilia put her up to this."

13

Alex had summoned Annabelle to meet with her alone and now she sat sternly waiting in her living area. Jess brought in a very subdued-looking Annabelle.

"Sit down," Alex commanded, as cold as she had ever been.

Annabelle sat and Alex looked at her. Pain was in Alex's eyes. She had never felt so betrayed in all her life. Perhaps the last time was when Annabelle had left young Alex to run away with Lord Delacourt. Loving Annabelle all those years ago and letting her in had given Annabelle the power to hurt her. And here she was, doing it all over again.

"I'm so so sorry, Alexand—" Annabelle started.

"Shut up." Alex cut her off short. "You'll answer my questions and you won't speak otherwise. I want complete honesty or you can leave right now." Alex's expression was deadly. Annabelle stopped talking and waited. "My main question, Annabelle, and I need you to be fucking honest with me here . . . I remember asking you to undress me and help me to bed. I definitely consented to that. Then I passed out, asleep. Did you touch me sexually at any point?"

"God, no, Alexandra. I'm not a sexual predator. I promise you on the lives of my children; I never touched you. I just made it look like we might have had sex."

"And then you told Erin and Vic that we *did* have sex. You told them that I came on to you, I believe."

Annabelle looked down at her hands and picked at the skin along the side of her perfectly manicured nails anxiously.

"Yes. I did. I am so very sorry for that."

"My mother put you up to this, didn't she?" Alex's gaze was stern.

Annabelle looked shocked, momentarily, as though she had underestimated Alex.

"Yes. How did you know?"

"I remembered how you used to get along so well years ago. Cecilia always loved you. She always said you were the perfect lady and she always thought you married extremely well."

Annabelle sighed deeply and shook her head.

"So, the idea was to break up myself and Erin? To stop the wedding?"

"Yes. I'm so, *so* very sorry, Alexandra."

Alex felt sorry herself. Sorry for having trusted Annabelle and for bringing her back into her life. Sorry for having enjoyed her friendship and letting a snake get close to her.

"How on earth did you think that would work? You know how good my relationship with Erin is. You know that she would never believe that for a second. You know we are right together."

Annabelle looked genuinely remorseful.

"I do know that. I don't know why I went through with it. Originally, I thought that it would be easy. I know how much you used to feel for me. Only the closer I got, the more I knew that you and Erin were perfect together and my plan had such a little chance of working."

"Originally? You mean that the whole thing,

from the first letter, was part of the plan? My mother put you up to that? Our whole friendship over the past few months has been a lie?" Alex's voice raised in frustration.

"No, Alexandra. It has been real. But, yes, originally, your mother put me up to it. To get close to you and to find a way to stop the wedding."

"Your thing with Vic? That was fake too? Just a way of spending more time here to get close to me?"

Annabelle put her head in her hands. "God, yes. No. I don't know. Kind of. It seemed like a good idea. But I'm not in love with Vic."

"Vic is probably my closest friend. She deserves so much better than you. If you care about her or me at all, you'll end it with her. If it isn't already over after your behavior last night."

Annabelle nodded her head in defeat.

"What did Cecilia offer you in return? What was betraying me for a second time worth to you?" Venom dripped from Alex's voice.

"She offered me her family's lake house in Surrey for me and my children. It turns out Rupert has found ways of screwing me financially in the divorce. His new girlfriend is pregnant. It is very likely that I am going to come out of this divorce very badly. I should have been smarter financially through the marriage, but honestly, I never thought I would actually leave."

Alex looked at Annabelle. The woman she had once loved. She felt utterly broken inside. Annabelle had found it so easy to betray her. For a house. A fucking house.

"Alexandra. I know you won't believe me, but if I could take back what I did, I would. The past few months have been the best months of my life, being able to be your friend. I might have come into this with a plan, but the friendship that grew was genuine; I swear."

Alex sighed deeply.

"I'm going to need you to leave now." Alex raised her eyes and called toward the door. "Jess!"

Jess's response was instant. She was instinctively tuned in to Alex's needs.

"Ma'am." The door opened and Jess appeared in the doorway.

"Please see Lady Delacourt out."

Annabelle looked forlornly at Alex. She looked broken herself and a tear fell from her eye.

"I'm so sorry, Alexandra."

"Goodbye, Annabelle." Alex turned and walked out of the french doors onto the terrace. It was a windy day and there was a light rain. The skies were dark grey and angry. She waited a minute, until she knew that Jess and Annabelle had left the room. Then she leaned her hands on the wide stone wall and looked out over the castle grounds, and she screamed loudly into the wind.

14

It was a miserable, windy, wet day and Erin and Vic were at the stables. They were there because Alex had wanted to be alone to see Annabelle. Then Alex had checked in briefly via text after Annabelle had left, but had asked to be left alone. Nicolas had gone to visit some friends in London.

Vic and Erin were working in neighbouring stalls in the big barn, separated by metal bars, brushing their horses, sheltered from the horrible day. They had given the stable girls the afternoon off. The horses were happy and warm, and had plenty of hay to eat. There was no need for the stable girls to stay.

Erin and Vic had agreed to poo-pick the

stables and to feed all of the horses at five-thirty, if the girls left all the feeds out in buckets with the names of the horses on them, and extra nets of hay for each horse for overnight. There were twenty horses, and Erin and Vic didn't want to get the feeds mixed up.

"How the fuck could she do that to Alex?" Vic asked.

"God, I don't know. I had felt that something was off with her for a while. But I wondered if it was just because of her history with Alex that I was extra protective. Alex's mother really is a piece of work, isn't she?" asked Erin.

"She's always been fucking horrible. I don't know how anyone could hate their child so much, especially Alex. She has always been the perfect princess. It is like: what more could Cecilia want from her? I think she has always been jealous of Alex. Even when Alex was small, she was like this beautiful, golden-haired angel child with the sweetest, most perfect smile. She was heralded throughout the press as the brighter future for the monarchy."

"It's evil. What she is doing to Alex now is evil. Vic, what are you going to do about your relationship with Annabelle?"

"Oh god, it is *so* fucking over. I mean, I know I was being dramatic last night, but I don't really care about what Annabelle has done to me. We were both just having fun and lots of sex, you know. Nobody was in love. But what she tried to do to Alex fucking kills me."

There was quiet for a minute, and the only sounds were the horses breathing and munching away on hay, and the falling of rain outside.

"I'm so sorry for being a drunken dick and driving us into the lake last night, Bodyguard. Thanks for, you know, saving us all."

Erin waited a second. She wasn't mad at Vic. More than ever, now, their friendship needed to stay tight. "It's alright, Drunken Dick. Of all the things that happened last night, your escapades were definitely overshadowed. Next time you are drunk, I'm sending someone from Security to babysit you, though. No harm done, anyway. Oh, except to the Range Rover. I wonder if they fished it out of the lake yet? That's a very expensive car you trashed."

"Fuck, I know. I'm going to have to pay Alex off at £5 per week for the rest of eternity." She laughed. "Also, I am *totally* hitting on Swoolia at the wedding."

Erin laughed. "Don't let Alex catch you!"

Thunder sounded in the sky and the rain fell more heavily. The stables were a warm cocoon.

"Fuck, Samson is still in the field. I know I said I would leave him out till later because he doesn't mind the rain and he is a really outdoorsy boy, but it's getting heavy and I can't leave him out in a thunderstorm." Vic put on her waterproof jacket and zipped it up.

"You want me to come with?" Erin asked.

"Nah, you're fine. No point us both getting drenched. If I'm not back in fifteen minutes, then I've drowned or been struck by lightning and will need rescuing."

Erin laughed. "Okay, deal."

Vic headed out of the barn into the wind and rain, and Erin felt glad she wasn't going too.

It was peaceful alone in the stable with Shimmer. Erin noticed that Shimmer's mane was getting a bit long, so she set to pulling bits of hair out to shorten it. Although people imagined horse's manes were usually trimmed with scissors, actually that often wasn't true. Manes were usually "pulled" using a comb and twisting a small section of the hair around it and then pulling it sharply downwards. It didn't hurt the horse. Most horses didn't even flinch when it was done. Erin got herself a stool to stand on and she set to work on Shimmer's mane. Shimmer just continued happily munching away on her hay while she did it. The horse must have found it relaxing and sometimes she even snoozed while Erin did it.

Erin found herself lost in thought, amazed at everything that was going on and hoping that Alex was alright.

Suddenly a figure arrived at the door to the stable. Erin didn't turn around, thinking it must be Vic.

That was quick, fetching Samson in. I didn't hear his hooves coming into the barn though...

Erin jumped when she heard a man's voice.

"I've got a fucking knife, so I suggest you shut up and listen to me." His voice was calm and threatening. Erin recognised it immediately. Lord Hugo. She turned around and stepped down off the stool. He was blocking the stable door. There was no other way out unless she scaled the seven-foot metal railings that separated Shimmer's stall from that of the horse next door. Which would have been possible, but which wouldn't put Erin in a much better position because he would soon be able to block that door—and the same with the three subsequent stalls before the end of the barn, and the big barn wall.

Water was dripping from him and a large kitchen knife glinted in the artificial lights.

"What do you want?"

"Not so brave now that I have a weapon, are you, Dyke?"

Erin stayed quiet and waited, looking for points of weakness, for a moment where she could attack and disarm him. The stable door, at chest height between them, was making it impossible for her.

"Our visit the other week was not a fucking joke, you know. You must end your relationship with the princess. You must not go through with this wedding. You wouldn't listen when we played nicely, so now we are doing things the hard way. Your choice, of course. I'm not fucking around here, Bitch. If you don't leave today, I will slash this pretty fucking horse of yours. I will slash its fucking throat and leave it to bleed out. If you don't leave tomorrow, I will do the same to that stupid, massive dog of yours. And if you don't leave the next day, I will do the same to you. I will slash your fucking throat and watch you die. Three chances. Can't say fairer than that, right?"

Erin felt her heartbeat racing and adrenaline surging. She moved to position herself between Hugo and Shimmer. She felt rage building inside her. No way would she let him anywhere near Shimmer or Audrey.

"What the fuck is wrong with you? I thought it was bad when you sexually assaulted Alex, and I am in no doubt that you would have raped her if I hadn't stopped you. Now you want to kill my animals?"

"And you. Don't forget, I *will* kill you too if you don't comply. Even if you up security, there will be a day when you are alone. When there is a moment, I will get you then. You will spend the rest of your life looking over your shoulder"

"If you touch Shimmer today, you will be arrested."

"Well first of all, you dumb bitches have no CCTV in or around this barn, so you will never be able to prove that I was here. And secondly, you think I am working alone? I can assure you I am not. And yeah. I would have raped the fucking princess. Show her what a real man is. I may still do it." He leaned forward over the stable door and his hand holding the knife lowered slightly. His eyes glinted black like coals. "I often fantasize about her screaming underneath me while I—"

Erin moved fast and slammed her body with everything she had against his arm with the knife, trapping it between her hip and the stable door. She felt a sharp pain on the side of her thigh, but it wasn't her screaming, it was him.

"Fucking Dyke Bitch!" he yelled.

Then as Erin watched, she saw Vic jump on his back, clinging like an angry koala, with her right arm tight around his throat.

"YAHHH!" Vic yelled like a banshee as she did it. Shock ran across his face as though he hadn't expected that.

"What the—?" he tried to yell, but Vic's arm restricted his voice. She looked like she was trying to choke him out, but Erin knew from the angle of her arm round his neck that Vic had no clue what she was doing. Nevertheless, it was slowing him down.

Erin took advantage of his disorientation and moved her body quickly, taking his thumb from the knife hand and pulling it sharply back. He screamed loudly. "You fucking bitch!" He dropped the knife and staggered backward, with Vic still clinging to him like a backpack. He was trying to wrestle Vic off him. She was shouting at him. "You fucking dick. You mess with us and you will get what's coming!"

Erin wanted to laugh. Vic was so serious. But now wasn't the time. Erin vaulted over the stable door and ran over to them. She slammed her right shoulder into his hip as though to tackle him and he fell over backward. She used his momentum to roll him straight onto his belly, with Vic somehow still in position, and she took his right arm with his injured thumb and wrenched it up his back, hard. She used her own bodyweight to help Vic pin him to the floor, and he screamed in pain as she forced his arm further up in an armlock. She knew she had him now. If he moved at all, she had complete control of him via the armlock.

Erin heard commotion in the doorway to the barn, and both she and Vic looked up.

It was the security team.

They moved quickly to take control of Lord Hugo as Vic and Erin peeled off him. Vic's eyes were wild and she smiled and raised her hand to high-five Erin.

Erin smiled and raised her own hand to meet Vic's.

"Oh yeah, we fucking got him. Don't mess with

us," Vic sang happily, as members of the security team lead Hugo away in handcuffs.

"Did you call Security?" Erin asked her.

"Yep, I fucking did. And, guess what I also did?" Vic looked mischievous as she danced across the barn. Erin spotted an iPhone propped up against a feed bucket. "I fucking filmed him. The whole thing. All his confession bit. Including the sexual assault bit and the threatening to kill you bit." She picked up the phone and checked the recording.

"Omigod, Bodyguard, look at this. It even has me jumping him. Oh, fucking yes! Look how awesome we look! Look at you hurdling that stable door!"

Erin laughed. "You were amazing...not bad for a Drunken Dick."

"Not bad at all," Vic said with a satisfied smile.

15

Lord Hugo had a broken thumb and a dislocated shoulder from the incident. He was arrested and charged. Vic's recording was crucial evidence. It looked like he would go to jail for a lengthy time for threatening to kill, threatening with a weapon, and sexual assault on the princess. Alex had decided to go after him for the sexual assault too. Both she and Erin gave statements to the police, and they did an interview on national television, detailing what had happened to them. Alex said she regretted not reporting the sexual assault in the first place, but that sometimes traumatic events can be so big and scary that they can take time to process. Erin spoke about what had happened in the stables and how Vic had helped her take him down.

The media went crazy for the stories. The popularity of Princess Alexandra and Sergeant Kennedy went off the charts during the week leading up to their wedding. Erin was a hero yet again, and Alex was brave and stoic, speaking about what had happened to her and the pressures she had felt to be with Lord Hugo—even though deep down inside, she had always known she was gay.

The public loved them and gave them their full support. Lord Hugo was a villain whom everyone could hate.

Erin's leg had been slashed by the knife during the incident, but it was not a serious wound. She had gone to hospital to have it checked. They had decided not to stitch it, and the wound actually started healing pretty well over the next few days by itself.

Alex didn't speak publicly about Annabelle. She was deeply sad about what had happened. She believed Annabelle's remorse, but she couldn't get past what Annabelle had done. She distanced herself, and Annabelle was informed that she wasn't welcome at the wedding.

Also kept quiet was any involvement by Queen Cecilia and Prince Arthur. Nothing could be proven on that front, and Alex knew they had to tread carefully. Everyone assumed that Lord Hugo, the jilted lover, was acting alone.

Alex was in the dressing room with Alicia, Natalie, Jess, Julia, and Nicolas—dressing for her wedding. Alicia had finished with hair and makeup. She had pinned an exquisite diamond tiara into Alex's hair. Then Natalie and Jess helped to get Alex into the dress. She looked at herself in the mirror. She looked incredible, regal and princess-like, but at the same time, like a fairytale. The delicate lace draped over her collarbones and arms, and covered her back where the dress dipped low. She couldn't imagine a dress being more perfect.

"Alexandra, you look magical. Sergeant Kennedy is a very lucky woman." Nicolas smiled at her.

"Ma'am, you look amazing." Jess and Natalie spoke at almost the same time.

Alicia smiled widely at her.

"So beautiful," Julia said, beaming with pride.

The women who worked so hard for her every day were looking at her with tears in their eyes.

Alex felt tears building in her eyes as well. "I never thought this day would come. I am the lucky one. I feel like I am living a fairytale."

"Maybe, you are," Nicolas said. "Maybe you are."

The ceremony was to be held in the big, central open area in the castle. In the rose gardens, at Alex's request. Luckily, the weather was beautiful and the sun shone brightly. It was everything a royal wedding never was, but everything that both Alex and Erin wanted. Although Erin would have preferred it to have been just the two of them, she recognized that marrying a princess involved a lot of people and a lot of publicity.

Everything looked magical and the garden was surrounded by television cameras, both low and high. The wedding was being broadcast live on all channels. The nation had been given a public holiday to celebrate the royal wedding, and people were hosting street parties throughout Great Britain. Nobody was working. Businesses closed down all over the country. Even those that had to go on working, like hospitals and police stations, had the wedding on—and staff were watching it when they could.

The king had decided it best that the queen and Prince Arthur attend the service, to avoid difficult questions being asked. They were to be placed at a distance from Erin and Alex, with a Close Protection Officer placed on each of them. Instead of being responsible for their safety, the Close Protection Officer was responsible for ensuring that they behaved. If anything felt even a little bit off, they were to be swiftly removed from the ceremony.

Alex walked down the aisle that had been created between chairs that were decorated with roses. The sweet scent of the roses encompassed everything.

So many guests were there. Her friends, whom she loved so much, and her close staff, whom she had insisted should be present.

Alex glanced sideways as she walked down the aisle, seeing Jess and Alicia clinging to each other, smiling and sobbing. All of her staff had been blown away when they had been asked to attend. It was unprecedented for a royal wedding.

She saw her father beaming proudly, with Julia

sitting on one side of him and Erin's parents on the other. Erin's mum waved madly at her.

Alex looked forward to see Erin smiling at her. She looked devastatingly gorgeous in a navy blue pant suit. Her George Cross medal was pinned to her chest. They had created a beautiful cravat made of ivory silk and the same beautiful lace that was on Alex's dress. Erin's makeup was simple and natural, and her hair was sleek and dark, and pinned back. Alex almost swooned, as though she was in a movie. She felt like she had to pinch herself. This was her real life. Her gorgeous partner, soon to be wife. Her fairytale.

"It is time for the vows. Princess Alexandra, would you like to go first?" The celebrant turned to Alex. They had written their own vows. Alex had spent ages thinking about it. She wanted it to be simple. She wanted this to be their moment. Time for just the two of them. It would happen in front of the eyes of the world, yes, but really it was just the two of them. She looked into Erin's eyes, took her hand and began.

"Erin, you came into my life at exactly the

right time. I had spent so many years hiding who I was, and it took meeting you to set me free. During our time together, I have had the happiest moments of my life, but also the most trying. These trials have pushed the boundaries of what we thought we could endure—but, my darling, with you by my side, I know I could endure anything." Alex saw tears forming in Erin's eyes. She continued, "You saved my life. Both literally, in the way that everybody has heard about, but also metaphorically. Before you, I was living a lie. I was a shell of a person. You have given me everything to live for. I love you dearly for all that you are, and all that you continue to give to me. You are my rock. As your wife, I promise to support you through it all, through the highs and the lows. I promise to share with you everything that I have and everything that I am. I want you to follow your dreams and I vow to always be right there beside you. I'll be your biggest cheerleader. Our love has an unbreakable strength. Knowing that, I promise to be by your side till the end."

Erin was crying and Alex squeezed her hand.

"Sergeant Kennedy, your vows?" The celebrant nodded kindly at Erin. Erin blinked the tears away, looked into Alex's eyes as though remembering that it was just the two of them, and began.

"Alexandra, before I met you, I never imagined in a million years that I would fall in love like this. My love for you was immediate and all-encompassing, and it has been the same ever since. Nothing about our journey has been easy. But the hard times have shown our strength and our resolve to always be there for each other. You are the princess the world knows and loves, and I promise to spend the rest of my life supporting you and serving you in that role, and beyond that when you become queen. You will always be a queen to me. Our marriage will always be public, but underneath it all, it's just about you and me. I will always support and protect you. I love you endlessly."

Alex felt herself welling up with tears as she felt the magic of the moment. It was just her and Erin underneath it all. She felt that deeply.

"You may now exchange rings and kiss the bride." The celebrant smiled at them both encouragingly.

The rings were passed to each of them by Nicolas, who had been deemed more responsible than Vic for the care of the rings. Alex took the platinum and diamond band and slipped it onto Erin's ring finger and Erin took a matching one and slipped it onto Alex's. Alex looked at her hand and smiled. The new ring sat neatly next to the big Kashmir sapphire. Alex felt her grandmother with her inside. She would have approved, becaues Alex had found her maharaja.

She felt Erin's hand cup the side of her face and she looked up at her stunning wife. Erin leaned down and kissed her, and Alex lost herself entirely in the kiss. She felt desire, passion and love for Erin slide through her all at once, and she knew she would never ever get enough of kissing Erin. Erin leaned Alex back over her arm dramatically during the kiss, as if they were in a theater production, and all of the guests went wild, cheering.

It felt like the beginning of something beautiful.

It <u>was</u> the beginning of something beautiful.

THE END

HER ROYAL BODYGUARD BOOK 4

Catch up with Erin, Alexandra, Vic, Nicolas and everyone else in Her Royal Bodyguard Book 4

You can get it at the following link: getbook.at/HRB4

Thank you so very much for reading these books. I really hope you enjoy reading these characters as much as I love writing them. I am overwhelmed with all the supportive and awesome messages and reviews. Thank you so much for buying my books and for supporting an indie author. My girlfriend, dogs, cats, and tortoise are very grateful too!

ALSO BY MARGAUX FOX

You can get a copy of my book, *Summer Love*, for FREE by signing up to my mailing list at the following link and keeping up with everything I am doing.

Click on the following link or type into your web browser to claim your free copy and to join my mailing list: https://BookHip.com/MFPGZAX

"An incredibly written tale about two amazing women and their illicit love that is so wrong, but oh, so right. Lily is astounding and intriguing in every way."

Pick up a copy of my hugely popular romance, *Lily's World*, where a detective falls for the criminal mastermind she is supposed to be investigating. It is available at the following link getbook.at/Lilysworld

If you missed it earlier, order Her Royal Bodyguard Book 4 at the following link getbook.at/HRB4

Thank you again for reading. I'm eternally grateful for your support in buying my books.

Do follow me on social media @lovefrommargaux

Printed in Dunstable, United Kingdom